The Magic Quirt

SELECTED FICTION WORKS BY L. RON HUBBARD

FANTASY
The Case of the Friendly Corpse
Death's Deputy
Fear
The Ghoul
The Indigestible Triton
Slaves of Sleep & The Masters of Sleep
Typewriter in the Sky
The Ultimate Adventure

SCIENCE FICTION
Battlefield Earth
The Conquest of Space
The End Is Not Yet
Final Blackout
The Kilkenny Cats
The Kingslayer
The Mission Earth Dekalogy*
Ole Doc Methuselah
To the Stars

ADVENTURE
The Hell Job series

WESTERN
Buckskin Brigades
Empty Saddles
Guns of Mark Jardine
Hot Lead Payoff

A full list of L. Ron Hubbard's
novellas and short stories is provided at the back.

*Dekalogy—a group of ten volumes

L. RON HUBBARD

The Magic Quirt

GALAXY
PRESS

Published by
Galaxy Press, LLC
7051 Hollywood Boulevard, Suite 200
Hollywood, CA 90028

Printed in the United States of America.

ISBN-10 1-59212-376-7
ISBN-13 978-1-59212-376-6

Library of Congress Control Number: 2007903540

Contents

FOREWORD — vii

THE MAGIC QUIRT — 1

VENGEANCE IS MINE! — 31

STACKED BULLETS — 61

STORY PREVIEW:
GUNMAN'S TALLY — 87

GLOSSARY — 93

L. RON HUBBARD
IN THE GOLDEN AGE
OF PULP FICTION — 105

THE STORIES FROM THE
GOLDEN AGE — 117

Stories from Pulp Fiction's Golden Age

AND it *was* a golden age.

The 1930s and 1940s were a vibrant, seminal time for a gigantic audience of eager readers, probably the largest per capita audience of readers in American history. The magazine racks were chock-full of publications with ragged trims, garish cover art, cheap brown pulp paper, low cover prices—and the most excitement you could hold in your hands.

"Pulp" magazines, named for their rough-cut, pulpwood paper, were a vehicle for more amazing tales than Scheherazade could have told in a million and one nights. Set apart from higher-class "slick" magazines, printed on fancy glossy paper with quality artwork and superior production values, the pulps were for the "rest of us," adventure story after adventure story for people who liked to *read*. Pulp fiction authors were no-holds-barred entertainers—real storytellers. They were more interested in a thrilling plot twist, a horrific villain or a white-knuckle adventure than they were in lavish prose or convoluted metaphors.

The sheer volume of tales released during this wondrous golden age remains unmatched in any other period of literary history—hundreds of thousands of published stories in over nine hundred different magazines. Some titles lasted only an issue or two; many magazines succumbed to paper shortages during World War II, while others endured for decades yet. Pulp fiction remains as a treasure trove of stories you can read, stories you can love, stories you can remember. The stories were driven by plot and character, with grand heroes, terrible villains, beautiful damsels (often in distress), diabolical plots, amazing places, breathless romances. The readers wanted to be taken beyond the mundane, to live adventures far removed from their ordinary lives—and the pulps rarely failed to deliver.

In that regard, pulp fiction stands in the tradition of all memorable literature. For as history has shown, good stories are much more than fancy prose. William Shakespeare, Charles Dickens, Jules Verne, Alexandre Dumas—many of the greatest literary figures wrote their fiction for the readers, not simply literary colleagues and academic admirers. And writers for pulp magazines were no exception. These publications reached an audience that dwarfed the circulations of today's short story magazines. Issues of the pulps were scooped up and read by over thirty million avid readers each month.

Because pulp fiction writers were often paid no more than a cent a word, they had to become prolific or starve. They also had to write aggressively. As Richard Kyle, publisher and editor of *Argosy,* the first and most long-lived of the pulps, so pointedly explained: "The pulp magazine writers, the best of them, worked for markets that did not write for critics or attempt to satisfy timid advertisers. Not having to answer to anyone other than their readers, they wrote about human beings on the edges of the unknown, in those new lands the future would explore. They wrote for what we would become, not for what we had already been."

Some of the more lasting names that graced the pulps include H. P. Lovecraft, Edgar Rice Burroughs, Robert E. Howard, Max Brand, Louis L'Amour, Elmore Leonard, Dashiell Hammett, Raymond Chandler, Erle Stanley Gardner, John D. MacDonald, Ray Bradbury, Isaac Asimov, Robert Heinlein—and, of course, L. Ron Hubbard.

In a word, he was among the most prolific and popular writers of the era. He was also the most enduring—hence this series—and certainly among the most legendary. It all began only months after he first tried his hand at fiction, with L. Ron Hubbard tales appearing in *Thrilling Adventures, Argosy, Five-Novels Monthly, Detective Fiction Weekly, Top-Notch, Texas Ranger, War Birds, Western Stories,* even *Romantic Range.* He could write on any subject, in any genre, from jungle explorers to deep-sea divers, from G-men and gangsters, cowboys and flying aces to mountain climbers, hard-boiled detectives and spies. But he really began to shine when he turned his talent to science fiction and fantasy of which he authored nearly fifty novels or novelettes to forever change the shape of those genres.

Following in the tradition of such famed authors as Herman Melville, Mark Twain, Jack London and Ernest Hemingway, Ron Hubbard actually lived adventures that his own characters would have admired—as an ethnologist among primitive tribes, as prospector and engineer in hostile climes, as a captain of vessels on four oceans. He even wrote a series of articles for *Argosy*, called "Hell Job," in which he lived and told of the most dangerous professions a man could put his hand to.

Finally, and just for good measure, he was also an accomplished photographer, artist, filmmaker, musician and educator. But he was first and foremost a *writer*, and that's the L. Ron Hubbard we come to know through the pages of this volume.

This library of Stories from the Golden Age presents the best of L. Ron Hubbard's fiction from the heyday of storytelling, the Golden Age of the pulp magazines. In these eighty volumes, readers are treated to a full banquet of 153 stories, a kaleidoscope of tales representing every imaginable genre: science fiction, fantasy, western, mystery, thriller, horror, even romance—action of all kinds and in all places.

Because the pulps themselves were printed on such inexpensive paper with high acid content, issues were not meant to endure. As the years go by, the original issues of every pulp from *Argosy* through *Zeppelin Stories* continue crumbling into brittle, brown dust. This library preserves the L. Ron Hubbard tales from that era, presented with a distinctive look that brings back the nostalgic flavor of those times.

L. Ron Hubbard's Stories from the Golden Age has something for every taste, every reader. These tales will return you to a time when fiction was good clean entertainment and the most fun a kid could have on a rainy afternoon or the best thing an adult could enjoy after a long day at work.

Pick up a volume, and remember what reading is supposed to be all about. Remember curling up with a *great story.*

—Kevin J. Anderson

KEVIN J. ANDERSON *is the author of more than ninety critically acclaimed works of speculative fiction, including* The Saga of Seven Suns, *the continuation of the Dune Chronicles with Brian Herbert, and his* New York Times *bestselling novelization of L. Ron Hubbard's* Ai! Pedrito!

The Magic Quirt

The Magic Quirt

GIT up, there, you, Mac! Gieup, Bessie! Carnsarn ye for a pair of busted-down, walleyed, spavined ignorantipedes! Gettin' so a man can't even git ten winks on his own chuck wagon without you buzzard baits clownin' up!"

Old Laramie curled twenty feet of whip into a powerful pop about their ears and the pair of swaybacks began to pull once more. The chuck wagon clattered and rolled over the last small hump and started down the curving, treacherous trail which led into and through Daly Canyon.

A horse is often wiser than a preoccupied man and Bessie or Mac might have had something to say if they could talk. For two wagons wouldn't pass on this narrow, precipitous trail. They let the whip pop away their caution and downward they shuffled.

Old Laramie had not liked being disturbed. It was just about dusk and shortly he would be elbow deep in the onerous duties of the cook of the Lazy G.

When the horses had shied and stopped he had been halfway through a little book titled: *THE SECRET OF POWER, A Twenty-Five Lesson Course in the Occult Sciences, Giving the Student Positive Control of His FELLOW MEN.*

That was for Old Laramie. By gad, if he didn't get some control over somethin' pretty soon he was going to turn Digger

Injun complete with breechclout and let 'em all go to the devil. For ever since Lee Jacoby had come as foreman to the Lazy G the life of Old Laramie had been worth less than a secondhand chaw of Old Mule.

"Hey, you cookie!" Lee Jacoby would howl. "Do you call this chuck, or did you make it to shoe horses with?" Or, "My Gawd, cookie, I didn't know you was a expert on mixin' poisons. Boys, we ain't got a cook, we got a apothecary! Throw it out and get me some ham and eggs."

It was the quality of the wit which injured. For as an old-time chef of the cow camps, Laramie was not unused to joshing. But ye gods, it ought at least to be funny. And it never, never, never ought to be followed up with dumping perfectly edible chuck on the ground.

The punchers of the Lazy G followed the leader. They weren't the old crowd. Ever since the Kid's pa got killed in Laredo, old hands had been drifting. First came Lee Jacoby with his cock-o'-the-walk brutality and then followed rannies who better suited the foreman's taste. They never consulted the Kid.

Young Tom Gregory had lost his mother when he was born and his old man when he was thirteen. And now at fourteen he was owner in title only, the Crawford County Bank—meaning old man Williamson—actually running the spread. It was all legal enough but things were happening. One of these days the Kid would have to drift, penniless. And Old Laramie was trying hard to stand by.

"By cracky," sighed Old Laramie, thumb in the book and

eyes vacant, "if I could do just one-sixteenth the things this Hindu feller says I can, I could run that Lee Jacoby plumb off'n the range. And Williamson to boot." He looked back into the book, read a moment and then growled with determination, "And the Bolger twins likewise!"

Rapt in this glorious dream, he didn't even begin to hear what was happening ahead. He drew an imaginary gun from an imaginary holster and said to the imaginary Gus Bolger, the same that had shot the Kid's pa, "Ye're powerless! With the magic wave of my left paw I creates you a statue! With a quick thumbin' of my right, I creates you a corpse!"

BANG! BLOWIE!

But it wasn't Old Laramie's imaginary gun. It was a real, honest-to-gosh shootin' iron. And Bessie and Mac recognized it as such, reared against the remorseless weight of the unbraked wagon, got shoved ahead, reared again and then, bronc fashion, scared to death, lit out like the Cannonball Stage straight down the curving road.

Whoever it was that had shot was not in sight. The road's curve hid him. But the speed with which Old Laramie was traveling would very shortly remedy that.

His old slouch hat whipped back in the hurricane and the chin thong nearly strangled him. He tried to grind home the brake shoe but he missed and had to use both hands and both feet to hold on. The reins were loosely tied to the brake and to reach them was impossible. He couldn't reach his rabbit's foot and his Little Jim Dandy Guaranteed Lucky Ring was carelessly left in camp!

Old Laramie once upon a time had been as tough as the next one, but three bullet holes, a sense of defeat and old age had ended that. He screamed like a wounded mountain lion and the scenery blurred by.

The chuck wagon finished the curve on two wheels, swapped to the other two, came back and tried to lean over the hundred-foot drop into the dry arroyo.

Straight ahead were six pack animals, clinging to the cliff beside the road as only burros can do. Directly in the track of the plunging wagon were two mounted men, holding guns on somebody or something out of Old Laramie's view.

But the horsemen weren't there long. They gave a white-eyed look at the cometing wagon and dug spur. Their outraged mounts reared and fought, to break away down the road in an uncontrolled run. The riders were out of sight and still going an instant later when Mac, tangling with a sideswiped burro, upset the chuck wagon entire, flat and loud in the middle of the road.

Old Laramie floated to an easy landing in sand and sagebrush. The sound of breaking crockery gradually ceased to echo in the surrounding arroyos. The dust dropped slowly down in the dusk.

Old Laramie spat, sat up, felt of his bones and then swore luridly and long. That seemed to relieve him somewhat and he looked at his horses. They were bruised but had struggled to their feet with no bones broken. The chuck wagon, however, had spilled everything from frying pans to cockroaches.

*Old Laramie floated to an easy landing in sand
and sagebrush. The sound of breaking crockery gradually
ceased to echo in the surrounding arroyos.*

"*¡Ah, gracias, gracias!*" wailed somebody. "*¡Gracias, amigo! ¡Gracias infinitas para todos mandados!*"

Old Laramie understood very little Spanish but he knew he was being thanked and he turned to find a small, fat Indian from over the line waddling up, bowing and advancing.

Three small children now rose wide-eyed from the sage and a woman, as fat as her man, came off a rock above the trail carrying a fourth child.

It was a very strange thing, thought Old Laramie. Sure these Mexican Indians didn't seem to be good bait for the owl-hoots.

The flood of Spanish went on with much flinging of the arms, and when it seemed that he was about to get kissed by the woman, Laramie got gruff.

"Hell, wasn't nothin'! Gimme a hand with this yere wagon."

They gave him a hand. The three kids picked up groceries and pans while the man and his wife aided to rig a block and tackle to right the wagon.

It was quite dark when the task was done and Laramie, less breakage, was ready to proceed on his way. He was getting mighty anxious when he thought of how Lee Jacoby would take this. For he should have been at Camp Seven something before supper time.

The little Indian was jabbering with more thanks.

"Quit it," said Laramie. "I would've done it for anybody. But just now I got to go."

"*¡Señor, su pago!*"

"Pago yourself," said Old Laramie genially. "But I got to go. I'm goin' to be roasted, clothes, hoofs and hide, as it is!"

The Indian was pulling forth a fat sack. From it he poured a small torrent of silver and gold coins. Laramie's eyes popped. So that was the bait! But he found that he was about to be paid. This unsettled him.

"Dang it, you ornery little cactus-eater. I didn't do you no favor on purpose. My horses run away and . . ."

The Indian tried to push the money at him but he finally succeeded in pushing it back. There was an immediate conference between the Mexican and his wife and finally the man went to the sad little burros and dug into a pack.

The thing which he now extended to Laramie glittered in the starlight. And the man made a valiant attempt at English.

"See! Thees theeng. *Látigo.* Make beeg man. *Muy fuerte* man, *látigo* he take. Beeg man make. *Muy fuerte.* Me not Indian. Me Aztec. You savvy? You keep. You beeg, beeg man. *Mucho* lucky. *Mucho!*"

Puzzled, Laramie took the object and found it to be a silver-mounted quirt. He was too anxious to get to Camp Seven to delay and so, saluting with the quirt, hastily got started before the thanks began again.

Mac and Bessie picked their way amongst the rocks of the canyon and soon came out on the flat where, in the distance, a fire marked the whereabouts of Camp Seven.

Laramie drew up beside the blaze and found Lee Jacoby standing there, eyeing him with his usual evil glare and perhaps something more.

Without palaver, Laramie got down, threw the back of the

wagon open and hurriedly began to throw cold beans and sowbelly in the direction of the blaze. Working so fast he was nearly a blur, he had supper ready for tin plates in less than fifteen minutes.

With an occasional grin and gibe the punchers jostled each other past and carrying their handouts and coffee mugs to nearby stones, soon ended the meal.

All this time Lee Jacoby had said nothing. The silence was worse than a tongue-lashing and when Laramie had handed the big black-eyed devil his chuck, the old cook shuddered. But still Lee Jacoby said nothing.

Later, when he was cleaning up, Laramie ruminated upon it uncomfortably and the Kid, coming up, had to speak twice before Laramie heard him.

"Oh, hello, Kid." He stopped and looked closely at the youngster. It was plain, even by the fitful firelight, that the Kid had been crying. "What's up, Kid?"

"Nothin', Laramie."

"Workin' too hard, mebbe?"

"Naw. Hell, it'd be a relief to work. I just rode out to see how things was doin' here."

"Somebody dress you down mebbe?"

"Naw. What do I care for these big stiffs?"

"Well, mebbe the bank, huh?"

The Kid was silent and quickly changed the subject. "That grub shore was welcome, Laramie. Ever since Sing Lee quit at the main ranch, I just about starve to death."

"Sing Lee? Come on, now, Kid. Why would he quit? By jumpin' sassafras, somebody . . ."

"Naw, Laramie. It just had to be that way, that's all. Williamson said a private cook for the owner might have been all right when my pa was alive but it was silly payin' a Chink just to feed one boy. It's the beginnin' of the end, Laramie. With stock disappearin' . . ."

"Kid, I been out in the camps for three solid weeks and today I was out of grub and had to go in to Crawford and that's as near to news as I been in a month. Why in the name of Beelzebub didn't you tell Williamson to go to hell? Why, if I'd been there—"

But he broke it off, suddenly ashamed. If he'd been there he would have done nothing. It was hell to have your nerve gone. There had been a time when he hadn't been Old Laramie. Young Laramie had been a gentleman to walk soft around. But that was before Bill Thompson. If he'd been there, he wouldn't have done a thing.

He got back to his dishes, the water raw and stinging on the scar of his gun hand.

The Kid started to dry on a flour sack. "Them damned Bolger twins rode through about an hour back," he said conversationally. "Seemed like they were in a hurry. Horses all lathered . . ."

"By the Eeternal!" cried Laramie, slapping his thigh. "By the Eeternal! Them's who it was!"

And he promptly told the Kid in confidence what had happened back in Daly Canyon. Nearly finished, he reached into the wagon and pulled out the quirt.

"Say!" said the Kid. "That's foofaraw!" And he turned it around in his hands. "What'd he say?"

"He said . . . hell, I never could get the hang of that spiggoty stuff. He said he was a Aztec and that this here thing would make me a big man."

"Aztec! Say, Laramie, there's an Aztec priest lives over by Blue Butte. Regular medicine man he is. Cave full of bats and stone idols. I been over there six, seven times but I never had nerve to go right up to the place. But one day nobody was home and I rid close by and peeked in. And say, it'd make your blood run cold. Stone idols with big green eyes. I bet he makes human sacrifices and everything."

Laramie looked wonderingly at the Kid and then at the quirt. For the first time he saw the design. The handle consisted of a coiled serpent whose head was the top and two great green eyes stared back at him. Suddenly he felt bewitched and thrust the gift from him.

"You're lucky he didn't put no spell on you," said the Kid, sagely. "I remember when Sing Lee almost jumped out the window when that old Aztec come up to the door. Sing Lee said he was a devil with an evil eye. If I was you, I'd put that away mighty careful. There's no telling what it might be."

Half-hypnotized by the green-eyed serpent, Old Laramie shoved it out of sight, he knew not quite where in the darkness. He had not the benefit, any more than the unlettered Kid, of a higher education which sternly forbade superstition. And besides, that snake was enough to give anybody the creeps.

The fire burned low and the punchers took to their sougans. And Old Laramie soon slept between the wagon wheels, wondering about what would happen to the Kid, wondering about why Lee Jacoby hadn't jumped him, and then tangling all in a series of dreams which culminated in a nightmare so horrible that it brought him stifled from out of his blankets, pawing for his foes, every hair erect on his head.

The fire was out and the night was still. A coyote answered another coyote and then a wolf, with a low, quavering moan, silenced all the lesser beasts. A gibbous moon cast a sickly light across the plains. It was still, it was lonely.

Old Laramie's heart quieted down and he sank back. But the bed was uncommonly uncomfortable and he twisted about for minutes before he finally investigated.

It was the quirt. He had shoved it into his blankets in error and on retiring had mistaken it for a rock. He whipped it out and it glittered in the moonlight, the two green eyes glaring at him.

"Make beeg man!" the little Injun had said.

Old Laramie scowled. But it was a funny thing about the quirt. It didn't seem to be so unfriendly now. As he looked at it a quietness stole over him.

Supposing, he sighed as he lay back and covered his head, supposing that was really true. Supposing that just by owning this quirt a man got to be big and powerful. That was a comfortable thought. Suddenly he sat upright and worked his blanket toward the tailboard. He reached up with a knowing hand and brought down one of his books.

He thumbed the pages in the unsteady light of a match.

. . . But amongst all other magical religions, that of the Aztecs was the most powerful according to record. Those tribes which lived in Arizona and New Mexico at the time of the Spaniards' coming were found to be in possession of much black magic, accounts of which have come fragmentarily to us from the early explorers.

It is said that some of these Aztec priests could produce howling storms at will and it was in one such that five men of the party of Juan Pérez perished. They had also the power of amulets and charms which, in their use, would protect the wearer against evil and create him a demon to his enemies.

It is stated in the Pérez Journal that by the use of such a charm one priest was able to withstand the shock of five Spanish troopers riding him down at full charge with lances. Unaccountably two of the troopers fell dead during the attack. The feathered serpent played a large part in the rituals of Aztec magic. . . .

Unsteadily Old Laramie grabbed the quirt. The flaring match showed him something he had previously overlooked. The serpent on the handle had feathers! Feathers which gleamed palely by the light of the gibbous moon.

Next morning, Old Laramie ladled out the hot cakes to the men with an air of grand disdain. It was early, still dark, and the punchers were either too sleepy or too hungry to notice. For once no one made fast comments on the quality of the food and when they came back for thirds Old Laramie banged down a lid and began to clear away. There was no argument.

The sun came up shortly after the last cayuse had been manhandled into servility for the day's work. Old Laramie stood around the deserted camp flicking his scuffed boot with the quirt and admiring the scenery.

How clean and clear it all looked! Funny, but the sky hadn't been as pretty as this to him for twenty years. Not since he was a kid riding range in the Panhandle. The crystal air was better than a jolt of bar whiskey and the sage smelled like perfume.

He sang contentedly as he strolled and so engrossed was he in the atmosphere that he didn't hear Lee Jacoby come up.

"Cookie!"

Out of habit Laramie turned in fright. But his new courage was too strong to be put down.

"Well?" he said stiffly.

"Get out to the holding corral and give the boys a hand with the wire. It's been cut in fifty places and we need help. Now get!"

Laramie looked coldly at the foreman. Flicking his scuffed boot with the quirt, he said, "Since when, Mr. Foreman Jacoby, does a cook mend wire?"

"Since now!"

"Well, Mr. Foreman Jacoby," said the old man with great dignity, "there's your chuck wagon and you know where you can put it. Me, I'm cuttin' me out a hoss and driftin' to town for amusement. I'll take fifty-seven dollars and twenty-nine cents wages here and now."

Jacoby blinked at the stern face. Suddenly he yanked a pad out of his levis and wrote a note with a pencil stub. This he threw at the cook. Without further conversation, Jacoby wheeled his bay and rode out of the camp.

15

Old Laramie grinned insolently. He gave the quirt a masterful spin and flicked the fallen note so that it rose to his hand.

Mr. Williamson:
Pay bearer $59 in wages. Also send me new cook today.
Jacoby at Camp Seven.

Laramie cut himself out a mean-eyed sorrel, pulled his saddle gear out of the chuck wagon and, with his worldly possessions on the cantle behind him, rode in great dignity due north across the flat to re-enter Daly Canyon.

He had gone about three miles and had just finished contemplating his scene of triumph in great magnification when hoofbeats rolled up the road behind him.

The Kid drew up beside him on a blowing American saddler.

"Gee whiz, Laramie. Gee whiz. You're not walking out. Gee whiz, you're the last man left of the old outfit! Come on, Laramie. Please don't do that. You don't know . . ."

"Sonny," said Laramie, "if you want to take a ride, come along into town and watch my triumph."

Saying which, Old Laramie produced a Colt .44 from thin air and blew a straggling cactus clean out of the ground. He whuffed the smoke from the barrel and slid the weapon into its holster.

"Gee!" said the Kid. And then worriedly, "What's up, Laramie?"

The old puncher grandly ignored the boy and they rode through the warming day toward Crawford. After a couple hours the false-fronts and 'dobe of the town shimmered into sight through the heat waves.

Laramie tied the mean-eyed sorrel up to the rail in front of the bank. "You wait here," he said, and, bowlegs creaking, waddled into the front door of the bank.

It was dim and cool in the interior and it took a moment for Old Laramie's ancient eyes to accustom themselves to the gloom. Finally he saw Williamson beyond the counter at a desk.

Without ceremony Old Laramie shoved through the gate and dug the note from his belt to toss it on the desk.

Williamson was looking at him oddly. The man was bald and fat and he hid a deal of craftiness under a large amount of false bluster. He seemed to have no bluster left, however.

Without taking his fascinated gaze off Laramie, he picked up the note. After a little he distracted himself enough to read the words. His hand shook a trifle and he got up hurriedly.

"Give this man his pay," said Williamson to the cashier. And then to Old Laramie, "Are you leaving town?"

"Don't reckon I will for a spell," said Laramie with a very tough scowl.

This seemed to give Williamson a great deal of reason to think. He retreated to his desk and sat there staring at Laramie. The puncher yanked his money to him and stuffed it in his belt. With one last truculent glare at Williamson he went out into the glaring sunlight and untied his sorrel.

"What's it all about?" blinked the Kid.

"Everything just goin' fine," said Laramie. He led his horse down the street to the Oasis Saloon and tied him up again.

The Kid tagged in after him, wondering if Laramie meant to go on a drunk. But Laramie passed straight on by the bar and came up before a faro layout.

The gambler was amusing himself in the deserted house by betting small sums against his own bank. He had had a good lunch and felt peaceful. He smiled woodenly at Laramie, very glad to have a customer who might, even this early in the day, attract others.

Laramie glanced at the picture of the tiger on the wall and then at the thirteen spades face up on the layout.

"Like to do some gamblin'?" said the dealer unnecessarily.

With a flip Laramie threw the gold piece on the bar. The dealer swept the double eagle into the till and advanced twenty dollars' worth of chips. He shuffled the deck, cut it and thrust it into the dealing box.

"Soda," showing in the deal box, was the ten of diamonds. Unreasonably, since there were only three more tens in that deck, Laramie tossed five dollars on the spade ten on the layout.

The dealer grinned inwardly, for here he was sure he had a fool whose money would soon be parted. He laid soda aside, his long white fingers sliding it smoothly out of the box. The six of hearts came to view. This, being the losing card, he slid out and placed beside the box. And as it slid, the ten of clubs came startlingly into view. The dealer permitted no sign of surprise to escape him. He paid the bet, kept the case on a board beside him, watched for Laramie to make his next bet.

He permitted, again, no sign of amazement. For Laramie let it all ride on the ten, to win.

Neatly, the dealer discarded the last winning card and disclosed the three of diamonds as the next loser. This he laid beside the box, starting a precise pile. He blinked ever so slightly. For there lay the ten of spades. There was just a hint of jerk in his hand as he tumbled out the chips.

He kept the case, saw that Laramie had left the whole pile on the layout ten and, with some slight impatience, discarded.

The next losing card was the three of spades and with a yank which he intended to be triumphant, the dealer pulled it and started to lay it in the neat pile. His hand halted midair. For the ten of hearts had been disclosed to full view.

Angrily the dealer thumped the chips down on Laramie's bet and by now the pile was spilling both ways. Laramie raked it all in, unsmiling, confident, and laid four blues before him.

"Now I think I will try aces," said Laramie.

The dealer permitted himself a private grin. He'd get that stack back. No fear of that. And so he put the discard aside, laid out the nine of clubs as the loser and then scowled blackly at the ace of diamonds which beamed at him from the deal box.

The chips nearly cracked as he paid the debt.

"Lettin' it ride?" snarled the dealer.

"Nope," said Laramie, matter-of-fact. "That next winner is goin' to be a two spot." And he bet eight blues to prove it. "And if you twist the deck around any, yore lungs shore could stand some ventilation."

The dealer discarded, disclosing the jack of spades as the

loser and then slipped this out to find the two of spades lying in full view.

The Kid understood very little of faro and cared less. He was uneasy at this change in his friend and, besides this, the sour smell of the saloon gagged him slightly. He wandered out into the street and watched two dogs fighting halfheartedly in the heavy dust of the road.

This was so slow that he glanced around for greater amusement and was rooted by the sight of Gus Bolger stepping out on the sidewalk before the bank, with Williamson at his elbow.

He knew it was Gus, for he was the smaller of the fraternal twins. The man's face was narrow, his visage dark, his eyes light gray and cold. Everything about him seemed stealthy and shadowed. Gus Bolger turned from the banker and waved covertly to someone across the street. Then, keeping to the wall, Bolger came toward the Oasis, hand resting on his gun butt.

The Kid trusted he had not been seen. He backed hastily into the Oasis and sprinted to the faro layout.

"Laramie! Gus Bolger is comin' in here!"

"Don't pester me, sonny," said Old Laramie with impatience. For he had just lost his first bet and though it had been small it bothered him. He was about to place his next and copper it to lose when the import of the Kid's message came into his brain.

He heard a light footfall in the door and whirled.

Gus Bolger stood, lightly balanced, leaning slightly forward, gun hand tense and still, at his side. "You there at the table. Come outside. I want to talk with you."

Laramie felt his heart start to climb and then the quirt brushed his leg. He steadied. "If yore so anxious to converse, I reckon this is as good a spot as any." He was aware of the dealer ducking into cover and the lone bartender vanishing behind the glasses on the bar.

"Come along here," snapped Bolger. "You wouldn't want to make trouble."

"I ain't makin' no trouble. But mebbe I'll unmake some. Say your say, Bolger, or draw—if yuh ain't too yeller."

The Kid was shaking as he moved to one side. He had no gun and his only friend in the world was about to leave it. For Bolger was known for these things. And the Kid's pa, though it was said in Laredo that the break was far from even, had been killed by this very man.

Bolger's hand blurred, his left stabbed down to fan. But he never connected with his hammer.

Three shots, tight together and loud as doom, shook Gus Bolger back, back, back.

Bolger, dead even as he fell, lurched into the window and fell sideways amid a shower of glass upon the boardwalk.

The last piece shook free from the arch which said "Oasis" and fell with one last musical tinkle.

With a quick sprint Old Laramie reached the body, gun ready just in case. But his last shot had been high and there wasn't any reason to suspect, from the look of the face, that Bolger would terrorize anyone again.

The Kid screamed, "Look out!"

Laramie dived sideways and a slug tore splinters from the walk where an instant before he had stood. Laramie wheeled toward the report, still falling sideways.

Across the street, Winchester raised and sighted, was Ray Bolger, striving insanely to get Laramie in his sights again.

But his horse was restive and shooting from the saddle was not good.

Ray Bolger dived out of leather and behind one of the fire barrels which lay at intervals in the street.

Laramie scrambled under a hitch rail and took cover behind the Oasis watering trough.

A slug struck a nail and glanced away with a shrill metallic yowl.

With an unsteady hand Laramie replaced the three empties in his .44. He saw the Kid hovering in the doorway behind him.

"Git out o' that!" he yelled.

The Kid dived back into the shadows and another slug broke the remaining window of the Oasis. But the shot had cost Ray Bolger his cover for an instant and Laramie took a snap shot at the exposed gun barrel and hand.

The shot was too tough and the next moment another bullet yowled away from the trough. A third drove through the corner and a stream of water jetted out to raise dust as it hit.

Laramie gripped the quirt. He looked behind him and saw a three-foot opening under the high boardwalk. Snake-fashion, keeping cover with the water trough, he went under the walk and, in its shadow, worked his way ten feet to the left.

Anxiously Bolger was seeking his enemy, exposing part of his face, then his shoulder.

Drawing very careful aim, the old cowpuncher sighted and let the hammer fall. The bullet glanced from the side of the water barrel and tore flying splinters away. Blinded and crazed with the pain of his lacerated eyes, Bolger sprang up and took the second shot, instantly following, squarely in the chest.

Laramie cautiously sidled across the street, eyes leery for another attack. He rolled Ray Bolger over with his foot. The man was breathing hoarsely.

There was a flurry of action in front of the bank a moment later. Williamson caught up the Kid's American saddler from the hitch rack, mounted and started to spur away.

Laramie blinked, saw the wild backward glance Williamson gave him which suddenly made sense.

He levered a new cartridge into Bolger's Winchester and very carefully laid his sights. The target was a hundred yards off but traveling straight away.

Laramie squeezed the trigger. He thought he saw the banker lurch but he did not fall and the saddler went streaking out of range.

The dealer and other citizens came out to cluster around the dead man and the wounded gunman. A doctor came shortly, still in his shirt sleeves as he had napped after lunch. He shook his head over Ray Bolger but had the man taken into the Oasis and laid on a pool table.

The Kid was standing popeyed before Laramie. Several citizens stood back at respectful distances and stared. Laramie took a long breath, hit his boot with the quirt and, with something like a swashbuckling air, went down to the sheriff's office to give himself up.

This gesture was not climaxed. For the sheriff was not there and a deputy, following discreetly, told Laramie in a courteous voice that he didn't have any authority, not having a warrant.

"The sheriff, he went out to check on some rustling," explained the deputy. "And he won't be back for a couple hours or so. Have a seat, sir."

Laramie sat down in the sheriff's chair, put his spurs amongst the scattered reward posters and built himself a cigarette. He was grandly unconscious of the citizens who, too late for the shooting, tried to look indifferent as they strolled by and stared in. Soon a knot of small boys had to be dispersed by the deputy, who came back, heartened.

"Sheriff's comin' up the road now. Got somebody with him, looks like. If you'll wait just a minute, he'll be right here."

The sheriff dismounted and, thrusting people to one side and the other, gained his office. He had already been told by only slightly coherent witnesses in the last ten feet that he had a big gunman in there waiting to give himself up.

"C'mon in, Lee," he called.

Lee Jacoby looked nervous. He glanced at the people, trying to make out what was going on and then, with a cinch on his nerve, started to walk in.

"Them Bolgers," said a loafer from the livery stable, "was just about the toughest customers we ever had in these parts. I reckon . . ."

Lee Jacoby stopped. He hesitated and began to back, hand on his gun.

"C'mon, Lee!" insisted the sheriff. "Why . . . what the hell . . . ?"

Laramie had gotten out of the chair at the first mention of Lee. He cat-footed to the door and there in the glaring daylight saw the foreman backing.

"Stop him!" cried Laramie, more lights dawning. "Stop him quick!"

Sheriff Quail never moved quicker than the spectators. He stepped to one side in the cleared lane, not knowing which man might be what. The deputy got himself a desk as a bullet backstop.

"Drop yore gun," yelled Laramie, "or I'll blow you in half!"

Lee Jacoby foolishly grunted in relief. He had been expecting at least a US deputy marshal. But Laramie . . .

"Stand where you be, Sheriff!" said Jacoby. "First man makes a move to stop me is a dead 'un!"

He had reached his horse and was about to mount. "Come down or I shoot!" yelled Laramie.

The old man never saw Lee Jacoby draw. There was flame and a smashing blow on Laramie's hip and another which spun him half around. He fell across the doorway.

"Next man that gets ideas gets the same!" shouted Jacoby and completed the mount.

He started to swing away, smoking gun covering them all, when three explosions almost together tore at people's nerves. The sheriff ducked back and when he looked again Jacoby's horse was running crazily at the boardwalk across the street and one Lee Jacoby was slowly falling into himself in the dust. The foreman's fallen gun was turning like a small pinwheel in the dirt.

After a while, when they had thrown a blanket over the body, they tried to pick Laramie off the walk. But he was not in a mood to be manhandled.

"Git off'n me! By gollies, it's gittin' so a man can't even rest without havin' a whole stampede making a trail of him."

They helped him to his feet and looked for blood. And there was blood. The slug had struck his cartridge belt, exploding two bullets which in their turn had given him flesh wounds in the left armpit. But even so, the bruises made it hard for him to walk.

"Sheriff," said the doctor, "Ray wants a word with you before he passes. . . . What's this? Another one?"

"It's Bunker Hill Day," said the sheriff grimly. He started to the Oasis.

"No," said the doctor, "he's in the Emporium. Said he didn't want to die in a saloon with his boots on. So he's in amongst the dress goods, if it makes any difference."

The Kid helped Old Laramie to follow and they found the dying gunman holding on hard to what life remained.

"All right, Bolger," said the sheriff. "What is it?"

"I got something to say. The old 'un . . . the old 'un got Lee, didn't he?"

"Dead center," said the sheriff.

"I ain't no Sunday-school boy, but I got my ideals," said Bolger. "Got any fault . . . fault to find with that?" he added belligerently.

"None," said the sheriff.

"Well . . . I tell you. I ain't goin' to Hell with murder on my soul. Gus is dead. Lee's dead and the sawbones says I won't be long. It was me who done in Tom Gregory, this kid's pa, in Laredo. Gus stood him up for a showdown and pretended to draw. . . . I shot him from an alley." He brooded for a moment and then, "He never even seen me.

"And it wasn't even because I didn't like him. He was always straight with us. So . . . so I got another score to pay off. It's Williamson. Go down and get him because it was him paid me and Gus to kill Gregory.

"Get Williamson. And hang him for murder. 'Cause he's killed Gus and Lee and Gregory, and all because he wanted money."

After a little he added, "Money ain't worth a damn compared to a man's life, is it?" He saw then that they knew he was crying because he wanted to live and the day was bright. "Get the hell out of here!"

"Wait a minute, Ray," said the sheriff. "You say Williamson did something. But what?"

Ray Bolger looked at him incredulously. "You mean . . . you mean you wasn't told? I . . . "

"What's what?" said the sheriff.

"Why, hell. Williamson was the one that hired us to kill Gregory. He put Lee in charge as foreman of the Lazy G and then he hired us to rustle stock off the Lazy G until he could force out young Gregory.

"We run the stock over the border. But a Mex's took it and sent the pay back by an old Indian. Aztec he said he was but I don't savvy too much Spanish. Gus did that. Used a bunch of kids and pack burros as a blind and came up here to tip us off for the next drive and to bring Williamson the pay they wouldn't trust to us.

"I . . . I don't savvy nothin'. But . . . anyway the old Indian wasn't satisfied with his cut. And he was blackmailing Williamson. So Williamson refused and sent me and Gus out to kill the blabber. But a wagon come down on us while we was doin' it and we dasn't stay. We thought we hit him but they wasn't no blood out there this morning and we couldn't find the Indian."

Bolger looked with agonized eyes at Laramie. "He . . . he didn't even tell you?"

"I don't speak no Spanish," said Laramie.

"Oh, my Gad!" wept Bolger. "All for nothin' . . . all . . . for . . ." He began to cough and Laramie turned away.

"Well, Kid," said Laramie, "you got your spread all set. Because what Williamson got paid will be adjoodicated to be your'n. And I guess I better go back to buckin' that tiger."

"Laramie," said the Kid. "Laramie, would you take the job of foreman? At a hundred and fifty a month?"

Laramie looked at the Kid and smiled. "Shore. Glad to. But now—"

"Old Aztec, huh," the proprietor of the Emporium was saying. "Who'd have dreamt it? Why, that fat old geezer and

28

his lardy wife used to come in here every couple weeks and sell me a lot of trash cheap. Like these."

Laramie turned, suddenly interested, and found that the storekeeper was holding up a very interesting item.

"Fancy, huh?" said the storekeeper. "All the big ranch owners across the border carry them. Mark of a big man. Two-fifty if you want one as a souvenir, Mr. Lara— But I see you've already got one."

Laramie was stricken.

"What's the matter?" pleaded the Kid, afraid.

The deputy came in to find the sheriff. "We got Williamson. He was plugged so bad he fell off about a mile east of here and a puncher brought him in. Let's— Hey! What's the matter with you, Mr. Laramie?"

But Laramie was past hearing. His eyes, resting on a rack of silver feathered-serpent quirts, fifty just like his own, began to glaze.

The amulet slipped from his fingers to the floor and Old Laramie, in a dead faint, sagged down on top of it, out cold.

Vengeance Is Mine!

Chapter One

H E knew, the instant he swung down from his dappled gray, that something was terribly wrong. Whitey was not much given to thought but to action. Behind him plumed four miles of his dust across the springtime desert. He rode like that even when his conscience did not bother him as it had today. He liked speed and he liked flash and a man who was everywhere acclaimed as Belleau Basin's best top hand was not much called upon to think.

Caroline was only an incident in his life where she would have been a life's whole purpose to a much less dashing man. But Caroline, as he and everyone else knew, would marry him some day, and Caroline often served him as a conscience.

She had said, "Whitey, it's been eight weeks since you've seen your pa. The snow's off the ridges and he'll be working hard at his claim. Ma Thompson's gone to town and you haven't another thing to do. Why don't you go see your pa, Whitey, just to make sure. He's gettin' pretty old."

And Whitey had said he guessed there wasn't anything wrong with that and he'd swung up and headed for the Long Jaw Fork where his pa was working this spring.

Conscience stabbed him like a spur when he looked at the desolation of the rickety camp. The raw red earth was unmarked by footprints and yet it had rained two days gone.

The big Long Tom was there but freshened currents had twisted it sideways and half wrecked it. And though it was noon there wasn't any smoke from the chimney. Little things, but they said a lot.

Old Hundred Bates, his pa, had been mining these hills, good luck and bad, for thirty-nine years. He'd chewed three fortunes from hard rock and blue gravel and he'd spent them with such lack of wisdom that he'd had to strip down to red underwear and chew again and again. And now the old man had gotten old. He'd spent the winter down at Gila Crossing, appearing in church every Sunday to insist on his favorite hymn, which had given him his nickname, appearing around the store weekdays looking forlornly up where the snow still lay on his newest strike. The old man was certain again that he'd die a mogul and be buried under an enormous shaft of granite and have solid gold on his coffin handles; meantime he was concerned about a grubstake.

Maybe it was because his ma had died in childbirth a month before her time because the old man was prospecting far afield. Maybe it was because Whitey had a conscience after all and really liked his father. He felt nervous and sick when he saw how deserted the cabin was.

His jingle bobs clinked as he gained the porch. That and the cry of a Stellar's Jay were the only sounds here. And yet there lay the old man's pack, empty and unwanted; he couldn't be far away.

Whitey leaned against a post and surveyed the yard, trying to guess where his father might be. The gray found some grass and yanked the reins out of his hand. Nervously, Whitey took off his hat and scratched his sleek blond hair. Not like pa to go roaming without pack or pick, nor let a Long Tom go askew in the creek.

Well, he'd leave the flour and bacon on the porch and sit himself down to wait. What if he was late getting home? His boss, Ma Thompson, he could kid and cajole into letting him do pretty much as he pleased, even if the spring roundup wasn't but half finished.

When he'd finished swinging the flour and bacon down from his saddle, he started to build himself a smoke, hat on the back of his head, brow furrowed in a frown. He couldn't find a match when he'd done and ducked in through the door and fumbled for one in the dim interior.

Whitey found his pa.

The old man was lying, still dressed, across his bunk and he'd been lying there for some time. His breathing had a rattle in it, a thing which was no mystery, for half his chest had been shot away. He'd bled the blankets black, and even if there was a spark in him, it needed no doctor to tell Whitey that his pa didn't have much time to live.

Whitey went down on his knees with horror in his eyes. There was no bleeding now, it was too late for that. His pa had been here for days. The heartbeat was feeble and the breathing caught, fluttered and caught again. A crow outside cried, "Bad! Bad! Bad!"

There was a streak of blood on the floor. There was a caked sample sack the old man had clutched to him on the bed but it hadn't stopped the bleeding.

Some consciousness of human presence came to Old

Hundred. He was too tough, had weathered too much to die easy. His eyelids flickered and he made an effort to speak. But his tongue was black with thirst which only the wounded know.

Whitey scooped water from the pitcher and slopped the cup as he put it to Old Hundred's lips. Ten feet from bunk to pitcher. God knew how long the old man had seen the white vessel on the table and knew what it contained.

The crow outside cried, "Bad! Bad! Bad!"

Old Hundred fainted and while Whitey stood irresolute, wondering how fast he could get a doctor there, the eyelids flickered again.

Old Hundred said, "Rich claim, Martha, rich . . ."

"Pa! This is Whitey, Pa. Who done this to you? Who done it?"

"Rich claim, Martha. You take . . . take the kids . . ."

"Pa, listen to me. This is Whitey. Ma's dead these ten years. Look at me, Pa. It's Whitey!"

This seemed to come home to the old man. "Whitey . . . Whitey, tell Martha . . ."

"Pa, who done this?" For it was plain to Whitey that he could never hope to get a doctor there in time.

"We'll make it again, Martha. Look on the beam over . . . over the stove. Three pokes . . . full . . ."

"Pa, this is Whitey. Look at me. Who done this, Pa? You answer me. Who done this?"

"Who . . . done this?" pondered Old Hundred, dying. Suddenly he fixed on Whitey. "You come, son." There was relief in it.

"Thank Gawd you know me. Who done this, Pa? Tell me."

Old Hundred coughed and drank a little from the cup and coughed again. "Whitey . . . you ride good, Whitey. . . . You shoot and ride good, Whitey. . . . You get Jess Stewart. . . ." He revived with false strength. "You get Jess Stewart, Whitey. You get him! Promise me you'll get him! Promise me!" There was ferocity in his convulsive grip and wilderness in his eyes. He yelled, "Promise me!"

"I promise," said Whitey, grimly. "How'd he do it? Why?"

Old Hundred started to speak again but sagged back, panting. The bleeding started once more. A man can last a surprising time with a shotgun shot in his chest, but Old Hundred was at the end of his time.

"Whitey, you tell Martha . . . three pokes. . . . Oh, Whitey, it's awful dark. Whitey! Whitey!" He began to cry and plucked around him. He found Whitey's hand and pressed it. "You tell . . . Martha . . . three . . . Whitey."

Whitey thought for a moment that the old man had drifted into a sleep. But it wasn't sleep for his eyes were wide and the rattle of breath was still forever.

For a long, long time, Whitey stood there. His pa that had carried him across streams and taught him to fish and ride and hunt, had made him be a puncher and not a miner because, "Somebody's got to hev money to bury me, kid."

"Somebody's got to hev money . . ." wept Whitey. And then he stood up and dashed the tears from his cheeks, mindful that a man grown shouldn't cry, mindful of other things and a promise.

It was the promise that put steel back into him. His mouth went tight and his fists clenched as he looked down at his pa.

He took the spare blanket and spread it over the ashen face and staring eyes and then he turned.

There was dust, gold dust, in a small pile on the stove. A lot of it. But there were three empty pokes on the floor and not a nugget in them. And the crow outside cried, "Bad! Bad! Bad!"

Whitey rode as though hell possessed him and the flanks of the gray were white and red when he came to the Triangle T.

Chapter Two

A rig was standing in the yard and Caroline was waiting at the gate. She'd watched him ride and knew it was no ordinary thing that brought him home with such speed.

His face was tight as he passed her. He was tall and straight and grim as he stood in the kitchen telling Ma Thompson.

"He was bushwhacked and I got to go," finished Whitey.

Ma had her bonnet off but her hands were full of bundles. She dropped them and a can of milk rolled unheeded under the table. "Whitey . . . Son, there's things men think they have to do and maybe that's right. But Mart Connelly's sheriff here and you're too young for murder."

"I knew you'd say that," said Whitey. "You wouldn't know. I promised him and he's dead."

"Who killed him?" said Ma, scared because she loved Whitey like the boy she'd failed to raise.

"I reckon I'll have to keep that, Ma. You'd tell."

"Somebody in the Belleau Basin?"

"A man I never heerd of until now, Ma. But I got to kill him for a snake that'd kill an old man for a few nuggets."

"Whitey. Sit down. Oh, it's you, Caroline. Get Whitey a cup of coffee. Now you listen to an old woman, Whitey. That's mighty dramatic, but it ain't good sense. You're young and killin' is killin' and it ain't for you. Mart Connelly's comin' here today to see about my boundary feud. You tell him and let him make a deputy of you and trail along. That's sense now."

Caroline's eyes were big and scared. She'd heard it from the porch. The cup and saucer rattled as she tried to obey her mother and give Whitey his cup of coffee. But he never looked at it as she set it down. He just stood and looked at Ma Thompson.

"I got to go," he said. "You wouldn't understand."

"Whitey . . . son. Please listen to an old woman. I know I ain't got good sense about a lot of things, but there's a phrase in the Good Book: *'Vengeance is mine, saith the Lord.'* Don't go agin the Book, Whitey. They'll hang you for a killer. Don't go."

"I got to go," said Whitey.

He put his hat back on his head and went to the bunkhouse for his sougan and war sack. He oiled up his gun and carbine very carefully. Then he cut his favorite, Rambler, from the remuda and saddled him.

Caroline was waiting at the gate. She had a sack of bread and meat and coffee and salt. Whitey wasn't seeing her at all when he took the food. She made the excuse that it wasn't tied straight on his cantle and fussed with the thongs.

"Don't . . ." she began and then stopped. This was a man's world and she couldn't break through. She knew what he'd think if she begged him to stay. She knew he might if he was begged hard enough. He had notions of courage and chivalry and vengeance for his kinfolk. She'd have to let him go.

"Don't what?" Whitey challenged.

"Don't stay away too long," said Caroline.

He rode away and didn't even look back at her. She knew she was wrong, then. He wouldn't have stayed no matter what she'd promise. There was dull misery in her soul for she knew she would never see Whitey again.

He had not cleared the lane when he encountered Connelly. Connelly was a rawhide frontiersman, a onetime Arizona Ranger, a man of reputation and very little to say.

"Howdy, Whitey," said Mart, for he couldn't miss the rider's preoccupation nor the sougan.

Whitey was suspicious. But he had to give the facts. He told them tonelessly and then tried to force Rambler by.

Mart was quick with a horse. There wasn't an opening in the trail now. "Who's the man he named?" demanded Mart.

"That," said Whitey, looking the sheriff straight through, "is between me and my pa."

"Where you goin', Whitey?"

"I'm goin' to take a trip. The country's too damned civilized."

"Who's the man, Whitey?"

"Go to hell."

Mart looked at the tall rider. "Whitey, if you go pluggin' somebody, revenge or no revenge, I'll have to take you in."

"That'll be then," said Whitey.

"And if you withhold material evidence now, I'm takin' you anyway."

Whitey looked dangerous and his gun hand trembled.

"I wouldn't," said Mart. "Not that you mightn't win. But you're a friend of mine, Whitey. Name the man and then you can go where you please."

The trail was blocked between the two strings of barbed wire. And no matter the urgency he felt, he couldn't shoot Mart even if he beat him to the draw. "Let me go."

"Name him," said Mart Connelly.

"Jess Stewart," said Whitey with a snarl. "Now get out of the trail or I'll ride straight through."

"Jess Stewart? Jess Stewart?" puzzled Mart. "I don't seem to recall . . ."

Being blocked on his way crystallized Whitey's determination. "Get outa my way, Mart Connelly."

"Now look, Whitey, the law . . ."

"To hell with the law! You'll dodder and fumble and spend months on a trial and then you'll let him go. To hell with the law, I say. What I got to do, I got to do, and you ain't got guns enough nor men enough to stop me. Get out of my way!"

Whitey stabbed spur and Rambler struck at the air with his front feet. Mart ducked and hurriedly pulled aside as Whitey at a dead run went away from there. Mart looked soberly at the wind devils of dust that marked Whitey's swift flight and then, shoulders sagged, went on up to the ranch from whence he could send word into town while he rode on to the claim.

Startled birds and rabbits flushed from Whitey's onward rush. Los Pinos grew laggardly large in the distance and the stretch of Rambler was all too short. He came plunging up to the Don't Care Hotel and Saloon and flung himself down.

Two of his friends were on the porch but he didn't speak to them. He went up to the dozing clerk and lifted him erect and staring from his tilted chair. The chair banged down.

"You know anybody stopping here name of Jess Stewart?"

It was hard for Tim, the clerk, to talk because his collar was so tight. He twisted away. "What the hell's got into you, Whitey?"

"Answer up."

"Who?"

"Jess Stewart. Him or any strangers in the past week?"

Tim scowled at Whitey and shrugged his coat on straight but he looked at the ledger and thought about it for a while. "Just a whiskey drummer and two women they wouldn't let stay. Nobody else for a month, Whitey. Them stages don't stop. . . ."

But Whitey was gone. Out in the street he saw Burt Landon and nodded briefly. Burt hauled water for people and got around.

"You know any strangers in the country named Jess Stewart—or named anything else?"

Burt was caught by the strained look in Whitey's eyes and the stiffness in his manner. He stopped his water wagon. "What's up, Whitey?"

"Just got to know, that's all. You get around. It's kind of important."

Burt gnawed at his mustache and shifted his reins. He thought for a long time, now and then eyeing the impatient Whitey. "Nope," he decided at last. "Ain't nobody but that widder woman and the two kids that come in to take over for Old Mrs. Greenbury on the Sixty-Six. What's up, Whitey?"

Whitey went on. He went on for two hours. He went on until he was heavy with exhaustion and nerves. But no one had heard the name that they could recall but said maybe if Jim, who was an old-timer and drove the stage . . .

Whitey put Rambler in the livery stable and was just pulling off his saddle when Holt, an old man whose body had survived the Indian days but who'd somewhere lost a part of his mind, came up to take a hand.

Holt was a peculiar man, not talking for days and then gabbing for an entire night without stopping. He talked to people who were not there and had been dead a very long time. The town tolerated him but walked a little wide and the young boys sometimes threw sticks and mud clods at him when he came out of his barn.

"I heerd you askin'," said Holt.

Whitey put the saddle on a rail and then suddenly recalled that Holt's memory was good for all his craziness and that people came to a livery stable. . . .

"I'm lookin' for Jess Stewart."

Holt started to rub down Rambler. "I heerd you askin', Jake."

"I'm Whitey, not Jake. I got to find a man."

"He ain't here," said Holt.

Whitey started to leave. But Holt added. "Not for fifteen year."

"You knew him?" Tensely.

"You're Whitey Bates."

"Yes."

"I knew him. He was a friend of your old man's. But they'd a fight and such. That was when yore ma and you was back East. He wan't here long and tain't likely he'll come back because that's the way with renegades. Leastwise squaw men.

44

Know how I knowed his real name? Had it on his saddlebag, inside."

Whitey felt dizzy. He steadied himself on a post. "What other name did he go by? What did he look like?"

"Quiet sort of feller. Bought a stud off'n me for twenty-one dollars cash. Sure saw him comin', I did. But the country was young. Warn't nobody around but miners and Injuns. Then she begin to settle and you and yore ma come up when Old Hundred struck it. Then these other people come. Had a squaw myself but they kilt her. Tribes was death on mixin' after the bad whites come. My old sidekick Happy Days says to me . . . Hello, Happy! I was jus' tellin' the boy here how 'twas 'fore she settled up. How you been?"

Whitey waited but the old loon rambled on to an unseen audience and no question would bring him back. Whitey finally shook him.

Holt stumbled to one knee and looked up, turned ugly. "You won't git no more off'n me. Everybody wants somethin' from me. They stole my land, the whites and the Injuns kilt her. Go on over to Rosarita and ask yore questions. Yore man ain't yere."

Chapter Three

W HITEY saddled, receiving no assistance. It was ninety miles to Rosarita and the day was already late, but he wasn't thinking about time or even about Holt. He was seeing Old Hundred and the water pitcher not ten feet away.

When he had Rambler out of the stall he mounted and ducked his head under the door beam. The brilliant afternoon sunlight blinded him for a moment and then he spurred swiftly out into the road and out of town.

Old Holt grinned evilly. "There's murder goin' iff'n I ever seen it, Happy. Murder goin' and a certain young man never comin' back. Well, that's what the country's come to. Come on in and have a drink." He laughed a little and looked back at the settling dust clouds.

The moon came up about nine o'clock, three-quarters full, painting the desert silver, showing the cactus blooms a startling white. It was spring and even cactus blooms in spring. The sage was fragrant and the wind was cool. The kerosene lights of Rosarita sparkled ahead, clearly seen from a dozen miles off in this crystal air. But Whitey had no eye for spring or beauty this night.

Rambler pulled up, blowing and weary, and Whitey, shedding dust motes into the porch light's glare, pushed his way into the largest saloon, the Single Strike. The interior made him blink, for the Single Strike had had cut glass sideboards and mirrors shipped all the way from St. Louis, and the Mexican bartenders kept things gleaming.

There were few there. A stud game was in quiet progress at the back. A drunk wept quietly into his whiskey at the bar. Two men of a certain rough stamp were at the other end talking in half whispers to each other over beer mugs filled with Mexican wine.

Whitey chose the bartender. He was a round little Mexican with a black mustache curled in points to his ears, an oddity in his race, of which he was quite proud.

"I don't want nothin'," said Whitey, "unless you've got water. I'm lookin' for a man named Jess Stewart."

The Mex shoved out some water with professional diffidence. "*No lo conozco, señor.* How do he look, this Jess Stewart?"

Whitey drank the water and looked up to find the pair at the far end looking at him strangely. He moved down the bar.

"Why'd you want to find him?" said the older one, beady-eyed under the dark brim of his Stetson.

Unconsciously, Whitey hefted his gun. "I got something to see him about. Is he here?"

The older one looked sideways at his friend and they both appeared uncomfortable. They seemed to have an unspoken conversation.

"He ain't here, kid, and he ain't been here for a long time. You better go home. If you got trouble for him, they'll only bury you."

Whitey's jaws went tight and he moved closer.

"Just friendly advice," said the older one. "You ain't likely to find many that'd sic you on."

Whitey was closer. "You better tell me where I can find him."

The older man moved out from the bar where he had room. "Sonny, I don't . . ."

Whitey had him by the coat lapels with such a savage twist that the man went down to his knees. The grip was strangling. Whitey's gun was covering the other man before he could fight.

"I don't want no war," said Whitey. "But if I don't find out where Jess Stewart is, there's no tellin' what I'll do. I got a reason." The older man was struggling, beating at Whitey's wrist with weakening, futile hands. The poker players looked up, curious but in no mind to interfere. The old one was a tough that rated a beating and the one that went with him was a punk.

"Don't kill him!" said the younger one, mad but scared, for the old man's face was turning bright red and then deepening to purple.

"Tell me!"

"He went to George Flats, damn you. Now let him go!"

Whitey released his man who dropped, coughing to the floor, beady eyes malevolent but powerless. He was badly frightened, for he had often supposed himself invincible.

Whitey holstered his gun and backed away. When he got to the doors he gave them his back and, untying Rambler, started to mount. He froze. Not sixty feet away, just dismounting from a white-lathered black was Mart Connelly. He was clearly seen in the glare of the Bird Cage Theater marquee, his face haggard, shirt and chaps dull with alkali. He seemed intent on the sheriff's office next door to the Bird Cage and for an instant Whitey thought he would escape unseen. Then Mart hailed him.

"Hey! Whitey! Wait! Wait, damn you!"

But Whitey wouldn't have waited for Gabriel himself that night. Rambler was tired, too tired to hear as he wheeled, but anxious spur sent the little cow pony frantically down the street and away from Mart Connelly.

Whitey rode hard and low. He knew this country indifferently well. George Flats was an old digging some leagues to the south, though just where he was not sure. But he did know . . .

There was a scream of urgency ahead of him and a man in a buckboard, seeing the hurtling rider too late, swerved off the road. But Rambler, weary and frantic, did not see the rear left wheel. He hit it and the sky spun and the earth struck Whitey.

For a few seconds he believed that he was pinned under the horse but found that he had unaccountably fallen backwards under the right rear wheel. He rose up, dazed and angry, and whistled for Rambler. It was moonlight but here the desert was of dark stones which showed no silhouettes and had not shown the wagon any more than it now gave him Rambler.

He whistled again. He'd trained the pony with his own hands for two long years. . . .

"What's the hell's the matter with you?" bellowed the driver. "Y've wrecked a wheel and kilt your hoss and all in bright moonlight. I've got a notion . . ."

"Hey! Whitey! Wait! Wait, damn you!"

Whitey froze. The thing he had thought was a rock was Rambler, Rambler with a broken neck.

It's a hard thing to lose an animal you love, that's carried you far and faithfully. But tonight was no ordinary night. There'd be time for grief. And he swallowed down the rising horror in his chest and threw a blue-glinting gun on the driver.

"Cut out a horse."

"Say. Are you crazy? These here is drivin' broncs and they'd go crazy. . . ."

"Cut one off the trace and hold him while I saddle. I'm placin' a twenty-dollar gold piece on your seat and that's ten times what he's worth. Do what I say."

The driver choked off further objections. He shrugged and unharnessed one of his horses, a buckskin with a hammerhead that rolled a wild eye when he felt the saddle blanket. The driver held him hard while the cinch was being drawn.

Whitey mounted up and quirted the horse into behaving. "I'll be back through here. What brand?"

"The Lazy B, but you needn't bother with that hoss."

"Where's George Flats from here?"

"Guess it's about due south. Mebbe a hundred mile, maybe less. Never been there but they say the country's awful dry. You better take this canteen. . . ."

But Whitey was already gone. He fought the hammer-headed buckskin every inch of the way throughout the night and the dawn found him worn and red-eyed in the saddle.

Chapter Four

IT was cold and he knew he would have to stop. The stars he guided by had faded and the sun's flat disk had not yet come. Moonlight had let him avoid canyons and sinks but now the dawn twilight was like blindness. A meadowlark trilled again and again to greet a fresh clean day.

Whitey got down. It was spring and there were wildflowers around a pool which would vanish when the summer's heat came. But up on the rim were century plants like a great barricade, saw-edged and waiting.

Whitey took a drink of water and bathed his face and wrists. The meadowlark flicked overhead and sat down on a nearby rock, painted by the morning sunglow.

Weariness plucked at him and told him to rest but Whitey would not let himself pause long. There was a terrible urgency in him, a fear that Mart Connelly would get there first.

Of course Mart would be slowed. He'd have to look around and ask to find the place where Whitey was going and he would probably have to get a fresh horse. Then there would be trails which would follow the water holes and that would eat up Mart's time. Whitey was a fast rider. He could make it. He yanked the buckskin away from the water before he foundered.

The buckskin fought to get at the pool. The rest had revived the devil in him and it took some time to mount. Sunlight was warming the air when Whitey finally made it.

He would not have been thrown at all had he himself not been so tired. But the bronc was cunning. He went away at a steady, bone-shaking trot and crossed the ridge. His rider lulled, the bronc suddenly stopped, humped and sprang skyward. He sensed that his rider was half off and he redoubled his efforts. On the third hop he had Whitey loose. Viciously, bawling victory, the mustang dropped him into the center of a maze of century plants.

Whitey screamed with agony as the spines bayonetted him. And then he dared not move. But he had to move, and when the shock had dulled, he tried to get free from the impaling swordlike leaves. It took a long time.

When he found the horse again, the lariat was dragging. The bronc cared more for water than he did for a human and, being stupid and groggy with cold drink, was caught.

It was agony to mount and hold the saddle but Whitey did. Broken spines dug into his back where he could not reach them, and his shirt and hat were gone. There was hardly an untouched place on his arms or chest. And the blood from his lacerated face was salty on his tongue.

He rode, heading by the sun, avoiding badlands, crossing flats where countless flowers bloomed, keeping his saddle.

He did not know his gun was gone until noon had passed and, for a wild instant, drew up in dismay. Then he saw the carbine in its boot and his eyes went hard again. He quirted the buckskin on.

They fled down shale slopes and over streams dying out even now before summer's approach. They skirted the shoulders of buttes and crawled, a tiny speck in the immensity of the brilliant desert. Day began to wane before he could be sure that they must be somewhere near their goal.

He mounted a bluff at sunset and with the last light saw a tiny cluster of huts ten miles to the west, pointed by three intersecting white trails.

Whitey took a grip on himself. Something was wrong with his coordination. The buckskin was half dead or the rider would have fallen once more at a sudden jump.

He looked at his arms. Here and there the purple and blue of the spines showed under his skin, broken and deep, and it came to him that the century plant was poison.

That shock steadied him. He sat up, mouth in a straight line and spurred down the slope toward George Flats. He was not scared. He would get his man and he'd get to a doctor. If they got the spines out and gave him some sort of antidote, he'd live. It was only if he didn't have attention, he told himself.

And then he was thinking of his pa and he took the carbine out and checked it as he rode.

The ten miles crawled under him. Things seemed to be going slower to him. There was a curious ringing in his ears and his heart lunged now and then as though it was trying to leap out of him. He'd get his man and he'd get to a doctor.

George Flats was poorly lighted. It was a poor camp, for the diggings had proved thin after the wild huzzah of discovery. Not more than a third of its buildings were occupied now and they burned frugal lights through unglassed windows. A Mexican colony lay to the north of the town and steer-fat cups flickered in the hovels around the bean patches.

Whitey was young and hard but he knew that his man had to be at George Flats. If he wasn't he had failed. He would have to see a doctor and rest. Perhaps he'd be sick for several days. Mart Connelly could not be far behind him.

Something like a sob came into his throat at the petty obstacle of pea vines on poles. He sawed the buckskin around them and stumbled through rubble into the town.

He sat for several minutes before the one saloon, unable to find strength to dismount. Then he carefully put a foot on the boardwalk and swayed with pain as he left the saddle and tried to stand. He locked his teeth and looked at the carbine by the flickering light of the sign, "The Nugget Palace."

A Mexican was sitting incuriously on the steps. Whitey focused on him and said, "You savvy Jess Stewart?"

The man hunched out of his serape a few inches and pointed inside. "He just enter, *señor*."

Strength, false and unlasting, came into Whitey's legs. He cradled the carbine and went up the steps. He let his eyes accustom themselves to the place before he stepped through the door.

Four men were at the bar. Two were miners, one was a gambler and the fourth was slender, very old with a softly haggard face. He was dressed in poor respectability and he took good care of his hands.

The four broke off when they saw Whitey.

He looked around. Only these four and a bartender. He took a deep breath.

"Which . . . which one of you is Jess Stewart?"

The fourth one with the fine hands set down his drink. He peered for a moment at Whitey and then, unbuttoning his vest and reaching very casually for something, stepped forward. "I am," he said.

"Then I'm killin' you for a murdering hound!" said Whitey.

The carbine roared. It shot again and the concussion made the lamps jump. It fired a third time but Jess Stewart was on his knees, gradually falling forward. He lifted up a hand toward Whitey as though in an appeal. But there was no appeal from the slugs in his lungs and throat. He fell forward with a dark shudder and from his hand rolled out a small, tinkling thing.

The three remaining at the bar had jumped away from the paths of the slugs. But they came forward now, staring down at Jess Stewart. They were very quiet as the gambler turned him over and felt gingerly through the blood for his heart. The gambler looked at Whitey.

One of the miners came forward and took the gun. Whitey was backed weakly against the wall, about to fall. The miner made no effort to help him.

From the dirty boards Whitey looked up at the faces which were gathering. "Get me a doctor," he whispered.

"Son," said the gambler with contempt, "you've killed the only doctor for a hundred miles."

Whitey felt the faces begin to spin and then carefully concentrated. "Get me a doctor."

57

"You killed him, you damned fool," said a miner.

There were hoofbeats in the street and just as the town marshal entered, Mart Connelly burst through the doors behind him.

"Where . . ." began Mart. And then he saw the thing under the pool table against the wall. He shoved the table over and he saw Whitey crowd aside.

"My Gawd, Whitey. I rode hard. I killed a horse. I tried, Whitey." He was kneeling, supporting Whitey's head. "This man is dying. He's half torn to pieces with cactus, can't you see. Where's a doctor?"

The crowd stood silent and unmoved.

"They say I killed . . . him," whispered Whitey.

"Get him some water!" demanded Mart and a bartender sluggishly complied. "I killed a horse getting here, Whitey. My Gawd, I found your pa's gun caught in a thicket. He'd pulled it after him and it went off. And I found his gold where the crows took it. Good Gawd, Whitey. You were raised here and you know the crows and rats. Why didn't I get here in time?" He looked his appeal at the crowd. "Get a doctor, somebody. Get some help."

The gambler was bleak. "Jess Stewart was the only doctor here, if that was his right name. He called himself Evans but he answered this kid. I won't help you. Jess Evans was a good man no matter what he done wrong in the East. He's give life back to a hundred people in this town. See this? It's a thermometer. Jess saw the kid was sick and he reached for his thermometer. He may have run with a bad crowd once but Jess never let a sick man down. And the kid, the kid that needs him bad, shot him down like a yellah dog. I won't help you, mister."

The shabby saloon was spinning and the desert night was reaching in through the door. It reached deeper and deeper, as deep as the things which Mart and the gambler had said. And then it reached all the way and Whitey slipped quietly and forever down.

He thought he heard Ma Thompson whisper, or maybe it was Caroline that was waiting at home. And the whisper said: *"Vengeance is mine, saith the Lord."*

It was very dark and cold.

Stacked Bullets

Stacked Bullets

THE whole town of Stud Hoss was worried stiff about the game going on in the Long Chance Saloon.

There is a certain system called *veintiuna*, a Spanish game of ill repute which demands that a man double his bets for each loss. The theory behind this is that one cannot lose forever. And if given unlimited resources the optimistic individual conceives that he can break any bank. However, there is a limit to any fortune, which, if coupled with a certain unwillingness of Lady Luck to smile, can lead only to the impoverishing of the most courageous optimist who ever got himself born, even if that one be Charley Montgomery.

In the dismal dusty interior of the Long Chance Saloon Charley Montgomery was competing, and disastrously, nine hours in the dark shadow of Lady Luck's back side. The game had started at one o'clock of a brilliant Arizona afternoon and while the solemn Joshua trees had fried about the little town of Stud Hoss, Charley Montgomery's smile had melted. The lines in his face had deepened. A brilliantly glorious sunset had blazed unnoticed. Darkness had fallen and soft moonlight had come to spread its deceptive glow upon the spotty grazing land of the Frying Pan Basin. But the three men in the Long Chance had no time for artistic appreciation of the glories of nature. They chose instead to rivet their gazes upon the glass-stained deal table, dingy and dirty below the smoky flame of the kerosene lamp.

Out of politeness the other worried denizens of Stud Hoss had steered wide. Discretion was the better part of their curiosity, for one did not intrude lightly upon the monomaniac pastime of Tate Coll, sheriff; Con Price, owner of the inner range; or Charley Montgomery. And so, much to the disgust of the half-breed bartender, the Long Chance had remained deserted. The violently intent trio formed an island of light within the fly-specked shadows of the rickety, sun-baked "Palace of Beverage and Fortune."

The three of them flicked the cards, bet, raked in winnings, shoved out losings and now and then grimly glared at one another. So deadly was this silent play that one of Con Price's riders passing by told the huddle before the harness shop down the street:

"By cripes, I never seed nothin' like it. That ain't no game, that's a duel. If I ain't missin' my guess one of them bunghole buddies is goin' to part from there as a corpse."

"Who's winnin'?" the harness-maker asked.

"Tate and Con," the rider told them. "There ain't enough chips in front of Charley Montgomery to buy a murder in Mexicali."

"That's irresponsible," said the harness-maker, setting down the tequila. "To my own perfect and complete knowledge Charley had nigh unto ninety thousand dollars at noon today. He might a hid his stake."

"Ninety thousand!" said the general storekeeper, coming up. "What the hell did he do, stick up the Reno stage?"

"Nope," said the harness-maker, authoritatively, "Charley is done sold out."

"The upper part of the blamed Fryin' Pan Basin," said a rider, "stock, barrel and longhorn, includin' the Chinese cook. Where the hell you been, George?"

The storekeeper looked at the yellow-lighted windows of the Long Chance and whistled. "And I thought that man had sense. Wealthiest man in the territory at noon and a saddle tramp at midnight."

"Oh, he ain't lost yet," said the harness-maker. "And I sure hope he don't. I wouldn't admire to make no coffins for Tate and Con. Charley's that bad with a gun that sidewinders die of pure fright when he so much as rides by. He won't take to losing his spread so easy. But then, hell, he ain't lost yet. Git up there, Bill, and see if you can hear what's goin' on."

"Who the hell did he sell to that had that much money?" said the storekeeper. "Now don't ask me that again, boys, I been up to Tucson for supplies. Ninety thousand bucks is a powerful lot of money."

"Charley don't seem to think so; the way he's tossin' it around you'd think it was confetti," said the harness-maker. "Well, who the hell do you think would have ninety thousand bucks on this range?"

The storekeeper's small watery eyes bugged, his mouth sagged, he grabbed the harness-maker by the arm and shook him. "Did *they* buy it?"

The harness-maker looked at him pityingly, shifted his chaw and spat into the moonlit dust. "Yep, you guessed it. The upper handle of the Fryin' Pan Basin and most of the

water holes is now in the complete and unscrupulous paws of
the Ringo twins. God help us. Though just how you come to
figure out, George, that they was the gents what transacted
this here transaction is plumb amazin' and does credit to your
gray matter. Boys, George here must of got awful smart on
his way up to Tucson. Wonderful what you can learn in a big
town. . . ."

The storekeeper was pale by the harness-shop lantern.
"Lord God, boys, what the hell'd you let him do that for? It
ain't like Charley Montgomery to sell us all out. Why, this
country won't be fit to live in for a hog. We'll be payin' for
water like pure runnin' gold. And who'll have money left to
pay my bills, that's what I want to know? I tell you. It's a sin
and a horror that you gents let this happen."

The harness-maker spat again. "George, how about you
makin' up a posse and goin' out to get them Ringo twins,
along with some of the boys? You got lots of reasons to arrest
them, mine robberies, border runnin', murder, and if you can't
exactly prove some of them why we still ain't got no doubts.
Now you just call up some of the boys and you take yourself
a posse—"

"Shut up! Confound you!" said the storekeeper, darting his
eyes between the patches of shadow among the false-front
buildings and down the street behind him. "Don't talk like
an idiot, this is serious. How in the devil did this happen?"

Several of the men in the crowd tried to tell him but the
harness-maker waved them to silence. "I don't blame Charley
Montgomery none," said the harness-maker, "and neither
should you. What with range wars and Texas fever he was

just goin' broke anyways. He's held on here through two or three years of drought just to please the rest of the ranchers down in the basin. You can't expect a man to go on like that forever. He ain't had no quarrel with the Ringo twins. They ain't never tackled him. Besides, it ain't wise to blame no man with that degree of skill with a shootin' iron. So, when they offered him ninety thousand bucks cash—"

"Stolen money," George exploded, "You know where they got that. And now what'll this range be like, everybody payin' for water from Willow Creek, nesters squeezed out, cattlemen bankrupt, banks busted, my store gone to hell. . . ."

He glared angrily at the Long Chance. "If Tate was anything of a sheriff he wouldn't let them damn Ringo twins—"

"Now, George," said the harness-maker, "you know dang well who caused the demise of the last three sheriffs we had in these parts. We ain't done nothing for old Tate to ask him to lay down his life for your store."

"What about Con Price?" demanded George. "Why don't he take his riders out and get them Ringo twins afore they settle down on the handle spread? If I was him—"

"Now, George, you ain't him," said the harness-maker. "If you'll just quiet down, George, we'll hear Bill's report on how that there game is going."

"Boys, he ain't got a blue chip left," said Bill. "My ma told me gamblin' was a sin. But I didn't believe it until tonight. What the hell ailed him to get in there with all that stake and git hisself cleaned out is more than I know."

"Maybe this'll make something I kin tell my grandchildren," said the harness-maker. And as he moved forward toward the windows of the Long Chance the crowd silently came with him.

Big, six-foot-six Charley Montgomery was down to his last white and this he slapped angrily on top of his two cards. "Stand," he said.

Con Price looked at him lazily, shifted his long legs under the table. He looked first at Charley's pat hand and then at Charley's blanched face. Tate had already taken two cards and was evidently standing on nineteen. Con turned over his own hand, face up, displaying a ten and a three. It was a bad hand to hit, but Con Price smiled slowly, confidently, looked at the back of the deck he held and flipped out a card. It was a six spot. He stretched and said, "Pay nineteen."

Tate's flat hand flipped over his two hidden cards and showed twenty. Con paid off.

But Charley Montgomery was on his feet. With a vicious thrust he threw the white chip into Con's face. "Take it and be damned to you," said Charley. "If I hadn't knowed you gophers sixteen years I'd swear that was a cold deck." But if he'd expected Con or Tate to draw on the accusation he was disappointed.

Con laughed slowly and drawled, "That's too bad, Charley. Can't say as I ever see'd such a run of hard luck afore."

"I saw Bat Masterson lose thirty thousand one night down in Dodge City," volunteered Tate.

"That ain't doin' me no good," said Charley. "Look, I got a saddle. It's a center-fire saddle, worth about two hundred dollars. If you gents'll let me I'll put it up for a hundred." Con looked at Tate.

"Think it's worthwhile?" Con asked.

"Mine's about wore out," said Tate. "I guess I been kinda heavy for it."

Con laughed. "Get your saddle, Charley."

Charley pulled his Stetson down and started for the door. When he got outside to the hitchrack he found that willing hands had already removed the riding gear and two men carried it back to the deal table for him.

"Pretty nice saddle," said Tate. "My roan will take that just right. Kinda pretty, though. If I ever run into outlaws they'll sure appreciate them glitterin' tapaderos. You could see a man on that for five miles."

Charley slammed down in the chair. "I'm plumb overwhelmed you like it, Tate. Deal the cards, Con."

"How much on one hand?" said Con.

"The whole thing. This run can't last forever."

Con shrugged. "You sure been playin' funny cards, Charley. I always figured this double every time you lose would break a man if he tried it. Now there you are throwin' your whole pot in. Are you sure you want to bet that saddle?"

"Shut up," said Charley. He tugged his Stetson over his eyes and hungrily watched the two cards coming to him. His big fingers trembled as he lifted their corners and looked and he could not prevent a triumphant gleam from springing into his eyes. Tate took three hits and went broke.

Charley patted the cards affectionately. *"Bueno,"* he said.

Con looked at his own hand which he had not before regarded. "Well, I'll be damned," he said, and carelessly turned over an ace and a jack. "Twenty-one, I guess that beats anything else that was on the boards, boys. What'll you give me for the saddle, Tate?"

With a long sigh Charley slumped down in the chair. He managed a feeble grin and then patted his pockets. One lone four-bit piece, the smallest coin in the territory, came to view. He looked toward the bar. "Drinks for the house. Well, Con, now I know what it feels like to be a saddle tramp. I knowed that ninety thousand dollars I had this noon was too good to last. I was goin' back East too, to buy me a big house and four-wheel carriages, get a swell gal and raise me some kids."

The half-breed, disregarding the four-bit piece, served three drinks. After Charley downed his he looked at Con. "What about givin' me a job, forty a month and bullets?"

Con shook his head. "Not for me you don't. I couldn't trust a man that careless with his money to do nothin'."

Charley flushed.

"Now, now," said Tate, "you just took this fine, Charley. But I tell you what I'll do. I'll point out a fact of how you can make a little money, namely one thousand dollars. And what with that and maybe a change of luck you can win back some of this stake. Maybe you could have your house after all, and the Mrs. and the kids. By God, though, I can't see a horn-toad like you in a hard-boiled shirt for the life of me."

Charley took Tate's drink and downed it. "Tate," he said, "for a thousand dollars I'd sell my grandma to the Pawnees." He looked around. "But ain't this kinda public?"

Tate shook his head, "Naw, Charley, what I got to say is strictly on the level. This here thousand dollars I'm talkin' about was entrusted to me by the Wells Fargo agent at Tucson to pay off any public-spirited hombre that might take it into his head to rid this here vale a tears of a couple of desperate characters."

"The way I feel right now," said Charley, "I'd take on Wild Bill Hickok single-handed with Billy the Kid shootin' at me from ten yards with a Henry repeatin' rifle. And while I don't go strong for this blood-money stuff, I figure I'm enough public-spirited to help you gents along all I can."

"What you got in mind, Tate?" said Con, lazily.

"Back about five or six years ago this was a peaceful country," said Tate. "Nothin' but Apaches and Mexican bandits and they wouldn't no more'n keep a man in practice on the draw. But then the horn-tailed gents that's overlords of this here infernal region done bestowed us a couple of prize members of the royal suite. After they'd shot up everybody that was shootable in Texas, blown an eight-mile swath through Kansas and formed boot hill associations all over New Mexico, the Ringo twins done decided to settle on us." His watery old eyes were watchful on Charley.

Charley had been fumbling with his gun; he thrust it solidly back into the holster now. "Tate, I thought you knowed my ethics better'n that."

"This ain't a question of ethics," said Tate. "It's a matter of cutting the wolf population of Arizona down by two. A thousand dollars would look mighty good in your paw right now, Charley."

"Tate," said Charley, "a man don't do business with a feller at noon and shoot him in the back at midnight. You ain't got nothin' to worry about. Them boys was wild, but then, shucks. Near everybody's wild when they's young. When I sold them the handle of this Fryin' Pan I made 'em promise clear that they'd leave off their evil ways and be a credit to this here thrivin' community of Stud Hoss. I already removed the menace."

Tate leaned back, fishing in his hip pocket. He sorted a slip of paper from between two plugs of tobacco and handed the stained remnant of writing to Charley who took it, puzzled over it with a deep frown.

"This don't make sense," said Charley. "It says: 'Warning to trespassers: It costs any a you gents that wants to water stock here five cents per head per month, payable cash in advance, until further notice.' What the hell, Tate? This is signed 'The Ringos.' Where'd you get it?"

"Old man Buchanan down at the print shop got it as an order for signs at three o'clock this afternoon. Them's goin' to be posted the whole length of Willow Creek. That's what you sold, Charley. You sold us all into bankruptcy. When the lower water holes go dry there won't be no place a man can take his stock but the south end of your old spread and with steers on the trail at four dollars a head, looks like the Ringo twins done bought the whole Fryin' Pan range. And the rest of us is gettin' ready to decamp to the nearest poorhouse. So they promised you to be good, did they?"

Charley looked at the paper and then put it aside. "Did you know about this, Con?"

"First I heard of it," said Con.

"Gents," said Charley, "you got to believe, I don't know anything about this. It never occurred to me that they might sell water. Hell, there ain't been no water sold in this country since the days of the Santa Fe Trail. They wouldn't do this—"

"The hell they wouldn't," said Tate, "And I got a thousand dollars reward right here in my pocket."

"Tate, are you sure—" began Charley.

"The dirty sons," said Con. "They pay you off with stolen money and then plan to run all your friends into bankruptcy. Who the hell would keep honor with such a pack of thieves?"

"Well," said Charley doubtfully, "They are violatin' what they told me but still— Look here, Tate, you got so much on these here gents, why don't you go out and bring 'em in?"

"I'm an old man, Charley," Tate sighed wearily. "And there ain't nobody in the valley would take on them Ringo twins, not considerin' the number of men they've killed. Besides, I got nothin' on them that would stand up in a court of law. All our best witnesses have been killed off. No, they got to be killed fair and square—in a nice legal gunfight. It's got to be self-defense for the feller that does it. There'd be investigations if the sheriff did it. Even if he had the nerve, which I ain't.

"But there's yourself, of course. You always said you never had nothin' on them or against them. Well, you got somethin' on them now."

Charley frowned for a little while. The hot light of the kerosene lamp beat down on his blond hair as he rumpled it with his fingers. "This here's a mighty delicate point, gents, but—"

"See here," said Tate, "I'll give you five hundred dollars of that thousand-dollar reward right now and you can go out and do the job when it pleases you."

Charley sat up with a jerk. He squinted at Tate and then at Con; he glanced around him for the two men who had brought in his saddle, recalling suddenly that one of them was a Mex who had been seen about with the Ringo twins. They had both vanished.

Charley looked around him carefully and turned till he faced the rear door. He motioned to the half-breed barkeep. "Lock the rear entrance, son." He sat back and shoved his cards at Con.

Tate dropped twenty-five twenty-dollar gold pieces on the table before him.

"Go ahead and deal," said Charley.

Con smiled slowly and riffled the cards. He burned the top one, dealt one to Tate, exposed a double eagle, and then hesitated.

"What are you bettin', Charley?" said Con.

"You see it," said Charley.

Con blinked and finished his deal. Tate took four irrational hits and went broke.

Charley squinted at Con and then looked at the deck. He scraped the edges of his cards on the table for a hit. A ten-spot, flat, fell silently in front of him. He looked at his cards and then looked at the ten. His head sagged a little and he turned up his hand. He had hit thirteen and was busted.

"How about the other five hundred?" said Charley.

Tate shook his head. "Not until you've delivered. You got the evidence. You got the reward. Personally I don't think you would have taken it if you hadn't been so damned anxious to

74

lose to Con again. But you've taken it and you've got your job. And if it's agreeable with you gents I think it's about time I hit the hay."

He filled his pockets with the bank-notes and gold and with a nod to Charley and Con went out the swinging doors. A minute later he came back in and picked up the saddle. He crowded through the curious onlookers outside with it and left.

Con dropped his pile into a soiled bandana and turned the corners. He tossed it to the half-breed. "Put this in the safe for me until morning, will you? Well, Charley, we've had quite a game, haven't we?"

"For you," said Charley. "Personally, I've been bored stiff. Hey, you, gimme another drink." He rose heavily, looked at the swinging doors and the crowded window and then walked to the bar.

"Come on, come on," said Charley. "Set it up."

The bartender looked indecisive. First, he knew Charley was broke, and second, and more important, at any minute the Ringo twins might call and fill this smoky air with singing lead. But Charley was an awful lot of man and not easily denied.

Shakily the bartender put a bottle of bar whiskey and a glass before Charley and turned to begin the hasty dismantling of the mirrors. They had been freighted in at vast expense from Santa Fe and were the only mirrors in Frying Pan Basin.

Charley took three quick drinks. "What the hell do you think of that?" he said. "Them dirty stinkin' coyotes breakin' their word not three hours after they give it to me. Relievin' Wells Fargo is one thing, and rustlin' cows is another, but when a man gives his word and don't aim to keep it, then he just plain ain't no good, that's all. Them Ringo twins would have to use a stepladder to get up to the level of a sidewinder's belly."

The bartender seemed to be standing in a semi-cataleptic fit, half in the act of lowering the last mirror. No muscle moved. His eyes had the unmoving stare of a dead man as he looked at a point just beyond Charley.

The recently ex-stockman paused, glass halfway to his mouth, and stood with a chill coursing up his back.

Methodically Charley set the glass down. And with great casualness he turned, keeping his hands well away from his guns.

Bert Ringo stood five feet inside the door. The windows and the porch were deserted of spectators. With a moan and a thud the barkeep disappeared.

Bert Ringo had his thumbs hooked in his belt. "I'm sure sorry to hear you say that, Charley," he said. "'Cause the only thing me and my brother uses to reach a sidewinder's belly is lead."

The yellow island of lamplight stood sharply ringed between them. The silence in the Long Chance became thick and deadly. "I ain't got no use for a broken promise," said Charley.

"The only kind of rustlin' we'll tolerate, Montgomery, is the kind we do ourselves. And now, if you'll oblige, we can step out into the street and get this over peaceful, with a minimum of name-callin'."

"No hard feelin's," said Charley. "Have a drink afore we go?"

"I don't drink with rustlers," said Bert Ringo. "Come on."

Charley shrugged and poured one for himself, then he thought better of it and left it on the bar. Stiff-legged and watchful, he started toward Bert Ringo, who held open one of the swinging doors for him.

"With you," said Charley.

Bert Ringo bowed and went out with him. Tom Ringo stood in the bright moonlight at the hitchrack. When he saw Charley appear he finished tying their horses and went out into the middle of the street.

"Shore is bright out here," said Charley. He looked up and down the row of false-fronts and found no sign of citizenry. "Shore is lonesome, too. Boys, I reckon you mean this to be fair and square and on the level. One at a time or both together?"

"I'll take it first," said Tom Ringo. "That's what you agreed, Bert. He's my man."

Bert shrugged. "Guess that leaves me to do the honors. Now if you two gents will just stand out here, back to back, when I give the word you can start walking. When you've gone fifteen paces I'll holler *stop*. Then when I say fire you'll both turn around and blaze away. Devil take the hindmost and no shots barred. Don't miss him none, Tom."

"Sure is decent of you gents to give me a break this way," said Charley. "I hope you understand there's nothin' personal in this."

Tom snorted. "Hear you lost the whole danged roll at cards. If you hadn't we'd be askin' for it back right now. If there's anything I can't stand it's a welsher."

"Don't be worried none about being broke," Bert said. "Me

77

and Tom will give you the best funeral money can buy. And that's more'n anybody else would do for a rustler around here. Take your positions, gents."

Charley took his gun out of the holster, made sure of the load, blew out the barrel, closed the side gate, and replaced it. "All set," he said.

They took their positions back to back, the bright moonlight throwing pale blue shadows from them. The coyotes barked lonesomely on the edge of town.

"Get ready," said Bert. "March!"

The chill of premonition was colder than the wind on Charley's face. His heightened senses reached eagerly to the beauty of the desert night, grasped the tang of the sage, the hot odors of leather and horses close at hand. He started walking.

Bert was counting loudly. "One! Two! Three! . . . Seven! Eight! Nine! . . . Thirteen! Fourteen! Fifteen! Ready!"

Charley stopped dead still. He tensed himself. And a split instance before the command to fire, he threw himself into the dust and rolled tumbleweed fashion under the wheels of a hay wagon which stood in front of the feed store.

Two guns were talking. He had known he would hear two guns. Bert had never intended to let Tom have all the shooting fun. And Tom had known it. It was a wonder that they had waited until the fire command had been given.

A bullet banged against the iron tire of a wheel above him and went crying away into the night. He quickly bunched himself into the far side of the wagon's shadow and, swiftly drawing, was ready to pick off his targets. But there he was at a loss. Neither Bert nor Tom could be seen.

*They took their positions back to back,
the bright moonlight throwing pale
blue shadows from them.*

He detected jinglebob on the walk on his side of the street and hastily turned to see Tom just taking refuge in the entrance of the feed store. He tried a snap shot and knew he had missed.

He speedily shifted his position and the white dust where he had just been was powdered with hammering slugs. Bert was across the street firing from over the back of one of his horses.

Charley knew he could not long withstand this crossfire, and made himself small among the wisps of hay which had fallen from the wagon.

The stillness was so deep it hurt the eardrums. The gunfire had stopped the yapping of the coyotes and even the wind seemed halted. The moonlight was pale on the dust of the street.

Charley heard a lucifer being struck. And a moment later a burning gun wad landed on top of the hay wagon. Charley got three shots at Bert as he exposed himself to heave the flame. And strained breathless cursing told him that at least one of the shots had found its mark.

When the horses had been unhitched from the hay wagon the tongue had been left turned sideways so that the front wheels were at right angles to their usual position. As the hay began to burn above him with a merry crackle Charley saw that he had little time to lose.

Standing with bent knees he pressed his hefty shoulders up against the feed store side of the wagon and began to heave. The thing rocked four or five times and then with a crash turned over, spilling the burning hay in the direction of Tom

Ringo. As it went Charley dropped to his knees and sent another shot toward Bert to keep him in cover. The chance shot was more successful than he could have hoped it would be.

Bert lurched out from cover, staggered, and fell prone across the walk, his arms dangling from the high boards like twin pendulums gently slowing down.

Charley turned with quick confidence to get a shot at Tom. The burning hay lighted the entire street and the smell and sight of it panicked the horses at the hitch rack so that they plunged and broke loose to charge noisily down the street and out of town. But there was no Tom behind them.

"Drop it, Charley," came from the walk above his head and he flung himself around the end of the wagon.

A bullet tore the flesh of his upper arm, another nicked his ear, and then he was in cover again. But his cover was burning and the sweeping smoke of it brought irritable tears to his eyes.

"Come out of there, rustler," shouted Tom, and a bullet scored Charley's right side. His position was untenable and he floundered through the flaming hay to get to the other end of the wagon.

Tom had dived down off the walk and in a sudden puff of smoke turned aside to clear his eyes. When he looked up again Charley was nowhere in sight. Quickly deducing his quarry's new position Tom leaped further out into the street, and brought down his Colt for a chop shot fair at the flame-limbed target.

Charley could almost see the shot coming. His gun jolted

twice in his hand and then something turned him around and the moonlight and flaming hay were all mixed up with the horrible spectacle of Tom Ringo trying to hold in his own blood with agony-clutched fingers. Charley saw Tom jackknife into the white dust and jerk stiffly. Then everything went out.

A little while later Charley found himself choking and coughing on a well-meaning but almost strangling glass of whiskey. He did not orient himself immediately but clutched for his gun and tensed as though to renew the battle. Tate gently held him down on the billiard table and Charley, more closely observing his surroundings, saw nothing but friendly faces above him and the scarred green cloth below him.

"Well," said Charley.

Con Price pushed away George, the storekeeper, who was extravagantly trying to give Charley another drink of whiskey.

"Both of them," said Con. "Goriest doggone gunfight I ever seen. Man, you were absorbin' lead like a bullet mold."

Charley winced under the ministering fingers of the doctor. "Anything busted or serious, Doc?" said Charley.

"Hell, no," said the doc. "You didn't even stop any of 'em. But you're going to look kinda queer with that notched ear. And some of these burns will hurt a while but they don't mean nothin' important in your young life."

Tate and Con Price exchanged a glance across Charley.

"Suppose the rest of you folks clear out and leave our friend here get a little air," said Tate. "Includin' you, Doc, if you're finished."

Unwillingly the crowd shuffled toward the door. The doctor put the instruments back in his bag, wound up a roll of gauze, and with instructions about rest and no whiskey, followed the crowd out.

"You lyin' easy now?" said Tate. Charley looked at them suspiciously.

"All right, I did what you wanted," said Charley, "Though I can't quite see how it all come about so sudden."

"There's a little matter we'd like to take up with you," drawled Con.

"Ain't I had matter enough today?" said Charley. "Made a fortune, lost it, killed two men. Looks to me like I been pretty busy. Supposin' you come around office hours tomorrow."

"This can't wait," said Tate. "Me and Con, well—we kinda got a heavy conscience, Charley. You got his gun, Con?"

Con had it.

"What the hell are you gettin' at?" said Charley.

"Well, I tell you," said Tate, scratching his half-bald head. "It seems to me like Con and me was kinda hard on you today. And we'd like to make up for it."

"Con and you? You won it fair and square," said Charley.

"Yeah, well, you see," said Tate embarrassedly. "We kinda thought . . ."

"We knew you had to sell," said Con, "And we didn't hold that against you none 'cause you'd a been bankrupt and it would of gone anyway if you hadn't sold. But me and Tate, well knowin' that you got a pretty peaceable nature—"

"And that you are sudden death with a gun," said Tate quickly.

83

"We knowed," continued Con, "you'd kinda have to be forced into this. And so, when you lost we kinda put it on strong—"

"And we run some of your stock off your handle spread this morning," said Tate, "knowin' this would kinda irritate the Ringo twins. 'Cause as soon as they'd start to take tally they'd see how much was gone. Well, you'll find that stock over in the south arroyo of Moonstone Canyon. A couple of my deputies is holdin' it there."

Charley started to rear up but Con pressed him back. Notwithstanding, Charley wriggled free. With some exclamations of pain and with a heavy frown he got off the billiard table, and, before they could stop him, grabbed the pack of cards which still lay under the kerosene lamp. He looked at the backs closely and interestedly. And shortly the story was told.

"Marked," said Charley. "Why you goldanged thieves. You steal my money and risk my hide—" He was turning purple in the parts of his face that weren't bandaged.

"We're goin' to pay it all back," said Tate hastily. "In fact, here it is now." And he quickly emptied both his and Con's winnings on the deal table. "It's all yours, every cent of it. And as I reckon the Ringo twins ain't got any heirs to speak of you probably better sell that handle spread of yours all over again."

"Maybe that's the way it looks to you," said Charley. "But it looks to me like you gents've shore been busy at my expense." Then he grinned and began to laugh. He looked from Tate to Con and laughed more loudly. "Well," he said, "I guess the joke's on me. You gents have shore relieved my mind. I thought my luck had gone for good. The very least you prairie dogs can do is get a new pack of cards and sit down here and cut for deal. Hey, barkeep!"

Story Preview

NOW that you've just ventured through some of the captivating tales in the Stories from the Golden Age collection by L. Ron Hubbard, turn the page and enjoy a preview of *Gunman's Tally*. Join easygoing Easy Bill Gates as he's forced to defend his ranch from evil landowner George Barton, who will stop at nothing to take his lands—including hiring the filthiest, fastest gunmen that money can buy.

Gunman's Tally

THE two horsemen streaked out of a patch of sage, one a length ahead of the other, dashed down the edge of a dry gulch and came streaming up the far side, leaving long curls of hot desert dust to unwind against the brittle heat of the day.

The man in the lead rode with teeth bared to the withering blast of his speed. His chin thong had bitten deep against his cheeks with the pressure of the wind against his stiff, straight-brimmed hat.

He loved his gray, that man, and yet his whip arm was never still as quirt rose and fell against the foaming flanks of his stretching mount.

The four-point rowels had left their many bright dots of red in the racing gray's flanks and jabbed now across the open to leave many more.

The alkali dust was in the rider's throat but he did not taste it. It was in his eyes but did not dim the fierce heat of his merciless glance.

He saw nothing of the red buttes before them, felt nothing of the sun's scorching, dehydrating ferocity. He was Easy Bill, on his way to Red Butte and to death.

He heard nothing of his companion's shouts. He had not yet realized that his companion was there.

Easy Bill Gates had forgotten his friend—he who would need so many friends in the short future.

But Jimmy Langman had not forgotten Easy Bill and he spurred his tortured sorrel through the melting-hot day, trying to keep in sight of the gray. Smiling Jimmy Langman was not smiling at this hour. He knew he would be needed, he would gladly have substituted himself. He had to keep up with Easy Bill.

"For God's sake, pull in!"

Smiling Jimmy's voice was thin and the racing wind whipped it back in his face with the dry sting of the alkali.

"You're killing your bronc!"

But Smiling Jimmy might as well have pleaded with the Joshua trees on the far horizon as with Easy Bill Gates that day.

The gray's heart was great, his stride was long. His speed had fattened Easy Bill's purse half a hundred times. But Easy Bill thought Buster, the gray, crawled that afternoon.

The ride was eternity. The way was infinity.

But Easy Bill would have ridden hellbent for China to meet Fanner Marsten. And Fanner Marsten was in Red Butte, a gun on each hip, a smile on his twisted face, waiting and watching for Easy Bill.

Jimmy Langman withheld his quirt to the last. Easy Bill flashed down a curving road strewn with black, smoking-hot lava stones, far in advance now.

Jimmy Langman let his quirt fall.

"Sorry, Mike," he told his sorrel and struck again.

"Sorry, Mike."

He dug his spurs.

"You understand, Mike. We got to be there with him."

The sorrel rushed down the stone-strewn road, breasting Easy Bill's dust, laying a smoke screen of his own.

Hoofs rolling, faster and faster. Hoofs thundering, louder and louder.

Fanner Marsten was waiting with a gun on each hip. Waiting for Easy Bill Gates.

Far off across the bleak waste, broiling between the coals of red canyon walls, Red Butte came into sight, twisted and shivering and squirming with the barrage of heat waves which shot skyward like a billion glass snakes toward the smoking bullion of the sun.

The gray was belly deep in the dust, reaching, reaching, reaching. The sorrel stretched out, shiny and white with lather, keeping up to the snare-drum rattle of Buster's racing hoofs.

"Take him, boy," pleaded Smiling Jimmy.

"Take him, boy."

"We got to be there when they draw."

Since the first instant he had glimpsed Red Butte writhing on its rack of heat in the canyon walls, Easy Bill had not once taken his eyes away from the miserable collection of weary, weathered buildings.

Fanner Marsten was waiting there with a gun on each hip and a smile on his twisted face.

Easy Bill's features were frozen by a glue of dust and sweat and hate. In all this withering, frying heat, his brain was frozen, a cake of ice, congealed around one thought—Fanner Marsten must pay!

Thundering hoofs, louder and louder. Heat waves above the town, taller and taller. The naked shame of the granite butte growing larger and larger.

Easy Bill was over his horn, his quirt arm was a steel piston he did not have to command.

Jimmy Langman's voice behind him went unheard.

"Wait, Bill. Wait! You're crazy! He's FANNER MARSTEN!"

Fanner Marsten must pay.

Fanner Marsten was waiting, watching, seeing this twin cumulus coming in a land where it never rained. Fanner was waiting with a score-notched gun on each slim hip and a smile on his bitter, twisted face.

Fanner Marsten on the high boardwalk was saying, "Here he comes, boys. That's Easy Bill. His funeral's on me!"

Easy Bill pushed back the canyon walls and thundered down the narrow pass. Jimmy Langman swerved around the turn behind him, quirt falling, young face drawn, blond hair white as lime from lather and alkali.

Something had to stop Easy Bill.

Something, anything . . .

"Wait!" cried Smiling Jimmy, his voice as hoarse and raw as a stamping mill. He swallowed the dust of his words as he cried, "Bill! You're crazy! He's FANNER MARSTEN!"

Something had to stop him this side of death. Something, anything . . .

To find out more about *Gunman's Tally* and how you can obtain your copy, go to www.goldenagestories.com.

Glossary

STORIES FROM THE GOLDEN AGE *reflect the words and expressions used in the 1930s and 1940s, adding unique flavor and authenticity to the tales. While a character's speech may often reflect regional origins, it also can convey attitudes common in the day. So that readers can better grasp such cultural and historical terms, uncommon words or expressions of the era, the following glossary has been provided.*

alkali: a powdery white mineral that salts the ground in many low places in the West. It whitens the ground where water has risen to the surface and gone back down.

American saddler: American saddle horse; composite of Thoroughbred, Morgan and Canadian breeds.

Arizona Ranger: a member of a group of mounted lawmen organized in 1901 to protect the Arizona Territory from outlaws and rustlers so that the Territory could apply for statehood. They were picked from officers, military men, ranchers and cowboys. With maximum company strength of twenty-six men, they covered the entire territory.

arroyo: (chiefly in southwestern US) a small, steep-sided watercourse or gulch with a nearly flat floor, usually dry except after heavy rains.

Billy the Kid: (1859–1881) a nineteenth-century American frontier outlaw and gunman, reputed to have killed twenty-one men, one for each year of his life.

Bird Cage Theater: also referred to as "The Bird Cage Opera House Saloon." This was a fancy way in the 1880s of describing a combination saloon, gambling hall and brothel.

blamed: confounded.

blue chip or **blues:** a poker chip having a high value.

boot: saddle boot; a close-fitting covering or case for a gun or other weapon that straps to a saddle.

boot hill: a cemetery in a settlement on the US frontier, especially one for gunfighters killed in action. It was given its name because most of its early occupants died with their boots on.

buckboard: an open four-wheeled horse-drawn carriage with the seat or seats mounted on a flexible board between the front and rear axles.

buckin' that tiger: bucking the tiger; the card game *faro* in which players lay wagers on the top card of the dealer's pack. Some early faro cards and layouts also displayed a portrait of a Bengal tiger, inspiring the term "bucking the tiger" to describe playing the game. In later years, a framed tiger portrait hanging outside a gaming house announced the presence of a faro game within.

bunghole: the hole in a cask, keg or barrel through which liquid is poured.

Bunker Hill: the Battle of Bunker Hill (June 17, 1775); the first major battle of the American Revolutionary War.

Three thousand British tried to take over the hill held by Americans. The first two attempts failed with the British ranks being cut to pieces and the hill strewn with bodies. The Americans ran out of ammunition and on the third attempt the British took the hill. The British won that battle; however 1,054 men were killed or wounded.

burn the top one: after the dealer shuffles and cuts, the top card is "burned" by showing it and placing it face up on the bottom of the deck.

Cannonball Stage: Cannonball Express; in 1901, the Cannonball Stage was started and continued to run until about 1913. It used six horses rather than four, and carried the mail as well as passengers. The Cannonball earned its name by "shooting" seventy-two miles in twelve hours, considered terrific speed in those days, with stops every ten miles for fresh horses.

cantle: the raised back part of a saddle for a horse.

carbine: a short rifle used in the cavalry.

carnsarn: consarn; damn; confound.

cayuse: used by the northern cowboy in referring to any horse. At first the term was used for the Western horse to set it apart from a horse brought overland from the East. Later the name was applied as a term of contempt to any scrubby, undersized horse. Named after the Cayuse Indian tribe.

center-fire saddle: a saddle with a single cinch rigged at the midpoint.

century plant: a plant with gray-green leaves up to 6.6 feet (2 meters) long, each with thorns on the edge and a heavy spike that can pierce to the bone. The leaves take ten to thirty years to mature and flowers just once before dying.

chaw: a wad of chewing tobacco.

Chink: Chinese.

chuck wagon: a mess wagon of the cow country. It is usually made by fitting, at the back end of an ordinary farm wagon, a large box that contains shelves and has a hinged lid fitted with legs that serves as a table when lowered. The chuck wagon is a cowboy's home on the range, where he keeps his bedroll and dry clothes, gets his food and has a warm fire.

cock-o'-the-walk: a chief or master; one who has crowed over or gotten the better of rivals or competitors.

cold deck: a deck of playing cards arranged in a preset order, designed to give a specific outcome when the cards are dealt. The cold deck is typically switched with the deck actually being used in the game in question, to the benefit of the player and/or dealer making the switch. The term itself refers to the fact that the new deck is often physically colder than the deck that has been in use; constant handling of playing cards warms them enough that a difference is often noticeable.

Colt: a single-action, six-shot cylinder revolver, most commonly available in .45- or .44-caliber versions. It was first manufactured in 1873 for the Army by the Colt Firearms Company, the armory founded by American inventor Samuel Colt (1814–1862) who revolutionized the firearms industry with the invention of the revolver. The Colt, also known as the Peacemaker, was also made available to civilians. As a reliable, inexpensive and popular handgun among cowboys, it became known as the "cowboy's gun" and a symbol of the Old West.

Colt .44: a .44-caliber, single-action, six-shot cylinder revolver, better known as the Peacemaker. The Colt Firearms Company, established in 1847 by Samuel Colt (1814–1862), made this version of their popular handgun to be compatible with the .44-caliber "Winchester Central Fire" cartridges used in Winchester rifles in the Old West.

copper it to lose: in faro, to place a copper token (traditionally a copper penny or later a six-sided token) on a card to lose. The player wins the bet if that card is the losing card in the deal.

cowpuncher: a hired hand who tends cattle and performs other duties on horseback.

coyote: used for a man who has the sneaking and skulking characteristics of a coyote.

cracky, by: an exclamation used to express surprise or to emphasize a comment.

cripes: used as a mild oath or an exclamation of astonishment.

Digger Injun: Digger Indian; an Anglo name for an Indian of the Southwest, Great Basin (between the Rockies and Sierra Nevada) or Pacific Coast. Most of these Indians were Shoshones or Paiutes. They were often called *Diggers* due to their practice of digging for roots.

'dobe: short for adobe; a building constructed with sun-dried bricks made from clay.

double eagles: gold coins of the US with a denomination of twenty dollars. They were first minted in 1849. In 1850 regular production began and continued until 1933. Prior to 1850, eagles with a denomination of ten dollars were the largest denomination of US coin. Ten-dollar eagles were produced beginning in 1795 and since the twenty-dollar gold piece had twice the value of the eagle, these coins were designated "double eagles."

false-front: a façade falsifying the size, finish or importance of a building.

fan: to fire a series of shots (from a single-action revolver) by holding the trigger back and successively striking the hammer to the rear with the free hand.

faro: a gambling game played with cards and popular in the American West of the nineteenth century. In faro, the players bet on the order in which the cards will be turned over by the dealer. The cards were kept in a dealing box to keep track of the play.

foofaraw: an excessive amount of decoration or ornamentation.

foundered: went lame.

Gabriel: the archangel who will blow a sacred trumpet or horn to announce Judgment Day.

G-men: government men; agents of the Federal Bureau of Investigation.

¡Gracias, amigo! ¡Gracias infinitas para todos mandados!: (Spanish) Thanks, friend! Infinite thanks for all you have sent us!

gray matter: brains or intellect.

grubstake: supplies or funds furnished a mining prospector on promise of a share in his discoveries.

hammer-headed: stubborn, mean-spirited (of a horse).

hard-boiled shirt: clean shirt; also called a "boiled collar shirt" as the removable collar was often boiled clean, separately, to allow for an extra day or two's wear. The collars were often stiff and uncomfortable because they were heavily starched.

Henry: the first rifle to use a cartridge with a metallic casing rather than the undependable, self-contained powder, ball and primer of previous rifles. It was named after B. Tyler Henry, who designed the rifle and the cartridge.

Hickok, Wild Bill: James Butler Hickok (1837–1876), a legendary figure in the American Old West. After fighting in the Union Army during the Civil War, he became a famous Army scout and, later, lawman and gunfighter.

hombre: a man, especially in the Southwest. Sometimes it implies a rough fellow, a tough; often it means a real man.

hoss: horse.

ignorantipedes: humorous variation of *ignoramuses*; ignorants.

jingle bobs: little pear-shaped pendants hanging loosely from the end of a spur (small spiked wheel attached to the heel of a rider's boot); their sole function is to make music.

Lady Luck: luck or good fortune represented as a woman.

lances: long weapons with wooden shafts and pointed steel heads, formerly used by horsemen in charging.

Laredo: a city of southern Texas on the Rio Grande.

lariat: a long noosed rope used for catching horses, cattle, etc.; lasso.

látigo: (Spanish) whip.

lit out: left in a hurry.

livery stable: a stable that accommodates and looks after horses for their owners.

Long Tom: in mining, a type of trough twelve to fifteen feet long and about two feet wide. Mainly made of wood, it has a metal bottom with a sieve and a riffle box at its end. It is placed on an incline to facilitate the water flow when washing the dirt through to find gold.

loon: a crazy person.

lucifer: a match.

Masterson, Bat: (1853–1921) a legendary figure of the American Old West during a violent and frequently lawless period. He was well known as a gunman and was also a buffalo hunter, US Army scout, gambler, frontier lawman and US marshal.

Mexicali: a city of northwest Mexico near the California border and east of Tijuana.

muy fuerte: (Spanish) very strong.

nesters: a squatter, homesteader or farmer who settles in cattle-grazing territory.

No lo conozco, señor: (Spanish) I don't know, sir.

Old Hundred: a universally sung hymn in the US that has been known from the first settlements. The first book printed in the English colonies was the Bay Psalm book, and the ninth edition of this book, printed in 1698, included the Old Hundred psalm tune.

Old Mule: a brand of chewing tobacco.

owl-hoot: outlaw.

plumb: extremely or completely.

poke: a small sack or bag, usually a crude leather pouch, in which a miner carried his gold dust and nuggets.

puncher: a hired hand who tends cattle and performs other duties on horseback.

quirt: a riding whip with a short handle and a braided leather lash.

rannies: ranahans; cowboys or top ranch hands.

remuda: a group of saddle horses from which ranch hands pick mounts for the day.

Reno stage: a stage line that ran from Oklahoma to Fort Reno.

rowels: the small spiked revolving wheels on the ends of spurs, which are attached to the heels of a rider's boots and used to nudge a horse into going faster.

saddle tramp: a professional chuck-line (food-line) rider; anyone who is out of a job and riding through the country. Any worthy cowboy may be forced to ride chuck-line at certain seasons, but the professional chuck-line rider is just a plain range bum, despised by all cowboys. He is one who takes advantage of the country's hospitality and stays as long as he dares wherever there is no work for him to do and the meals are free and regular.

Scheherazade: the female narrator of *The Arabian Nights*, who during one thousand and one adventurous nights saved her life by entertaining her husband, the king, with stories.

¡Señor, su pago!: (Spanish) Sir, your payment!

serape: a long, brightly colored woolen blanket worn as a cloak by some men from Mexico, Central America and South America.

shootin' iron: a handgun, especially a revolver.

sidewinder: rattlesnake.

sinks: depressions in the land surface where water has no outlet and simply stands. The word is usually applied to dry lake beds, where the evaporating water has left alkali and other mineral salts.

slouch hat: a wide-brimmed felt hat with a chinstrap.

soda: the first top card turned face up at the beginning of a faro game, and is not used, but discarded.

sorrel: a horse with a reddish-brown coat.

sougan: bedroll; a blanket or quilt with a protective canvas tarp for use on a bunk or on the range.

sowbelly: salt pork; pork cured in salt, especially fatty pork from the back, side or belly of a hog.

spavined: suffering from, or affected with, a disease of the joint in the hind leg of a horse (corresponding anatomically to the ankle in humans) where the joint is enlarged because of collected fluids.

spiggoty: a Spanish-speaking native of Central or South America who cannot command the English language. It is a mocking imitation of "no speaka de English."

squaw men: white men who marry Indian women.

stamping mill: a machine that crushes ore.

steer-fat cup: fat lamp; a simple candle made by filling a shallow dish with fat or oil and adding a wick.

Stellar's Jay: a bird native to western North America that is closely related to the blue jay, but with a black head and upper body.

Stetson: as the most popular broad-brimmed hat in the West, it became the generic name for *hat*. John B. Stetson was a master hat maker and founder of the company that has been making Stetsons since 1865. Not only can the Stetson stand up to a terrific amount of beating, the cowboy's hat has more different uses than any other garment he wears. It keeps the sun out of the eyes and off the neck; it serves as an umbrella; it makes a great fan, which sometimes is needed when building a fire or shunting cattle about; the brim serves as a cup to water oneself, or as a bucket to water the horse or put out the fire.

tapaderos: heavy leather around the front of stirrups to protect the rider's foot.

Texas fever: a fever caused by ticks and spread by the immune but tick-infested cattle of the southern country to cattle of more northern latitudes. The prevalence of this fever was greatly responsible for stopping the old trail drives.

tongue: the pole extending from a carriage or other vehicle between the animals drawing it.

trace: either of two lines that connect a horse's harness to a wagon.

two spot: two-spot card; deuce card in a deck of playing cards.

veintiuna: (Spanish) twenty-one, also called *blackjack*; a card game in which the winner is the player holding cards of a total value closest or equal to, but not more than, twenty-one points.

walleyed: having large bulging eyes.

war sack: a cowboy's bag for his personal possessions, plunder, cartridges, etc. Often made of canvas but sometimes just a flour or grain sack, it is usually tied behind the saddle.

whiskey drummer: a traveling salesman who sells whiskey.

white: a white-colored chip having the lowest value, chiefly used in poker.

Winchester: an early family of repeating rifles; a single-barreled rifle containing multiple rounds of ammunition. Manufactured by the Winchester Repeating Arms Company, it was widely used in the US during the latter half of the nineteenth century. The 1873 model is often called "the gun that won the West" for its immense popularity at that time, as well as its use in fictional Westerns.

wind devils: spinning columns of air that move across the landscape and pick up loose dust. They look like miniature tornados, but are not as powerful.

L. Ron Hubbard
in the Golden Age
of Pulp Fiction

*In writing an adventure story
a writer has to know that he is adventuring
for a lot of people who cannot.
The writer has to take them here and there
about the globe and show them
excitement and love and realism.
As long as that writer is living the part of an
adventurer when he is hammering
the keys, he is succeeding with his story.*

*Adventuring is a state of mind.
If you adventure through life, you have a
good chance to be a success on paper.*

*Adventure doesn't mean globe-trotting,
exactly, and it doesn't mean great deeds.
Adventuring is like art.
You have to live it to make it real.*

—*L. RON HUBBARD*

L. Ron Hubbard
and American
Pulp Fiction

BORN March 13, 1911, L. Ron Hubbard lived a life at least as expansive as the stories with which he enthralled a hundred million readers through a fifty-year career.

Originally hailing from Tilden, Nebraska, he spent his formative years in a classically rugged Montana, replete with the cowpunchers, lawmen and desperadoes who would later people his Wild West adventures. And lest anyone imagine those adventures were drawn from vicarious experience, he was not only breaking broncs at a tender age, he was also among the few whites ever admitted into Blackfoot society as a bona fide blood brother. While if only to round out an otherwise rough and tumble youth, his mother was that rarity of her time—a thoroughly educated woman—who introduced her son to the classics of Occidental literature even before his seventh birthday.

But as any dedicated L. Ron Hubbard reader will attest, his world extended far beyond Montana. In point of fact, and as the son of a United States naval officer, by the age of eighteen he had traveled over a quarter of a million miles. Included therein were three Pacific crossings to a then still mysterious Asia, where he ran with the likes of Her British Majesty's agent-in-place

L. Ron Hubbard, left, at Congressional Airport, Washington, DC, 1931, with members of George Washington University flying club.

for North China, and the last in the line of Royal Magicians from the court of Kublai Khan. For the record, L. Ron Hubbard was also among the first Westerners to gain admittance to forbidden Tibetan monasteries below Manchuria, and his photographs of China's Great Wall long graced American geography texts.

Upon his return to the United States and a hasty completion of his interrupted high school education, the young Ron Hubbard entered George Washington University. There, as fans of his aerial adventures may have heard, he earned his wings as a pioneering barnstormer at the dawn of American aviation. He also earned a place in free-flight record books for the longest sustained flight above Chicago. Moreover, as a roving reporter for *Sportsman Pilot* (featuring his first professionally penned articles), he further helped inspire a generation of pilots who would take America to world airpower.

Immediately beyond his sophomore year, Ron embarked on the first of his famed ethnological expeditions, initially to then untrammeled Caribbean shores (descriptions of which would later fill a whole series of West Indies mystery-thrillers). That the Puerto Rican interior would also figure into the future of Ron Hubbard stories was likewise no accident. For in addition to cultural studies of the island, a 1932–33

LRH expedition is rightly remembered as conducting the first complete mineralogical survey of a Puerto Rico under United States jurisdiction.

There was many another adventure along this vein: As a lifetime member of the famed Explorers Club, L. Ron Hubbard charted North Pacific waters with the first shipboard radio direction finder, and so pioneered a long-range navigation system universally employed until the late twentieth century. While not to put too fine an edge on it, he also held a rare Master Mariner's license to pilot any vessel, of any tonnage in any ocean.

Yet lest we stray too far afield, there is an LRH note at this juncture in his saga, and it reads in part:

"I started out writing for the pulps, writing the best I knew, writing for every mag on the stands, slanting as well as I could."

Capt. L. Ron Hubbard in Ketchikan, Alaska, 1940, on his Alaskan Radio Experimental Expedition, the first of three voyages conducted under the Explorers Club flag.

To which one might add: His earliest submissions date from the summer of 1934, and included tales drawn from true-to-life Asian adventures, with characters roughly modeled on British/American intelligence operatives he had known in Shanghai. His early Westerns were similarly peppered with details drawn from personal experience. Although therein lay a first hard lesson from the often cruel world of the pulps. His first Westerns were soundly rejected as lacking the authenticity of a Max Brand yarn (a particularly frustrating comment given L. Ron Hubbard's Westerns came straight from his Montana homeland, while Max Brand was a mediocre New York poet named Frederick Schiller Faust, who turned out implausible six-shooter tales from the terrace of an Italian villa).

Nevertheless, and needless to say, L. Ron Hubbard persevered and soon earned a reputation as among the most publishable names in pulp fiction, with a ninety percent placement rate of first-draft manuscripts. He was also among the most prolific, averaging between seventy and a hundred thousand words a month. Hence the rumors that L. Ron Hubbard had redesigned a typewriter for faster keyboard action and pounded out manuscripts on a continuous roll of butcher paper to save the precious seconds it took to insert a single sheet of paper into manual typewriters of the day.

That all L. Ron Hubbard stories did not run beneath said byline is yet another aspect of pulp fiction lore. That is, as publishers periodically rejected manuscripts from top-drawer authors if only to avoid paying top dollar, L. Ron Hubbard and company just as frequently replied with submissions under various pseudonyms. In Ron's case, the list

A MAN OF MANY NAMES

Between 1934 and 1950, L. Ron Hubbard authored more than fifteen million words of fiction in more than two hundred classic publications. To supply his fans and editors with stories across an array of genres and pulp titles, he adopted fifteen pseudonyms in addition to his already renowned L. Ron Hubbard byline.

Winchester Remington Colt
Lt. Jonathan Daly
Capt. Charles Gordon
Capt. L. Ron Hubbard
Bernard Hubbel
Michael Keith
Rene Lafayette
Legionnaire 148
Legionnaire 14830
Ken Martin
Scott Morgan
Lt. Scott Morgan
Kurt von Rachen
Barry Randolph
Capt. Humbert Reynolds

included: Rene Lafayette, Captain Charles Gordon, Lt. Scott Morgan and the notorious Kurt von Rachen—supposedly on the lam for a murder rap, while hammering out two-fisted prose in Argentina. The point: While L. Ron Hubbard as Ken Martin spun stories of Southeast Asian intrigue, LRH as Barry Randolph authored tales of

romance on the Western range—which, stretching between a dozen genres is how he came to stand among the two hundred elite authors providing close to a million tales through the glory days of American Pulp Fiction.

L. Ron Hubbard, circa 1930 , at the outset of a literary career that would finally span half a century.

In evidence of exactly that, by 1936 L. Ron Hubbard was literally leading pulp fiction's elite as president of New York's American Fiction Guild. Members included a veritable pulp hall of fame: Lester "Doc Savage" Dent, Walter "The Shadow" Gibson, and the legendary Dashiell Hammett—to cite but a few.

Also in evidence of just where L. Ron Hubbard stood within his first two years on the American pulp circuit: By the spring of 1937, he was ensconced in Hollywood, adopting a Caribbean thriller for Columbia Pictures, remembered today as *The Secret of Treasure Island.* Comprising fifteen thirty-minute episodes, the L. Ron Hubbard screenplay led to the most profitable matinée serial in Hollywood history. In accord with Hollywood culture, he was thereafter continually called

The 1937 Secret of Treasure Island, *a fifteen-episode serial adapted for the screen by L. Ron Hubbard from his novel,* Murder at Pirate Castle.

upon to rewrite/doctor scripts—most famously for long-time friend and fellow adventurer Clark Gable.

In the interim—and herein lies another distinctive chapter of the L. Ron Hubbard story—he continually worked to open Pulp Kingdom gates to up-and-coming authors. Or, for that matter, anyone who wished to write. It was a fairly unconventional stance, as markets were already thin and competition razor sharp. But the fact remains, it was an L. Ron Hubbard hallmark that he vehemently lobbied on behalf of young authors—regularly supplying instructional articles to trade journals, guest-lecturing to short story classes at George Washington University and Harvard, and even founding his own creative writing competition. It was established in 1940, dubbed the Golden Pen, and guaranteed winners both New York representation and publication in *Argosy*.

But it was John W. Campbell Jr.'s *Astounding Science Fiction* that finally proved the most memorable LRH vehicle. While every fan of L. Ron Hubbard's galactic epics undoubtedly knows the story, it nonetheless bears repeating: By late 1938, the pulp publishing magnate of Street & Smith was determined to revamp *Astounding Science Fiction* for broader readership. In particular, senior editorial director F. Orlin Tremaine called for stories with a stronger *human element*. When acting editor John W. Campbell balked, preferring his spaceship-driven tales,

Tremaine enlisted Hubbard. Hubbard, in turn, replied with the genre's first truly *character-driven* works, wherein heroes are pitted not against bug-eyed monsters but the mystery and majesty of deep space itself—and thus was launched the Golden Age of Science Fiction.

The names alone are enough to quicken the pulse of any science fiction aficionado, including LRH friend and protégé, Robert Heinlein, Isaac Asimov, A. E. van Vogt and Ray Bradbury. Moreover, when coupled with LRH stories of fantasy, we further come to what's rightly been described as the foundation of every modern tale of horror: L. Ron Hubbard's immortal *Fear*. It was rightly proclaimed by Stephen King as one of the very few works to genuinely warrant that overworked term "classic"—as in: *"This is a classic tale of creeping, surreal menace and horror. . . . This is one of the really, really good ones."*

L. Ron Hubbard, 1948, among fellow science fiction luminaries at the World Science Fiction Convention in Toronto.

To accommodate the greater body of L. Ron Hubbard fantasies, Street & Smith inaugurated *Unknown*—a classic pulp if there ever was one, and wherein readers were soon thrilling to the likes of *Typewriter in the Sky* and *Slaves of Sleep* of which Frederik Pohl would declare: *"There are bits and pieces from Ron's work that became part of the language in ways that very few other writers managed."*

And, indeed, at J. W. Campbell Jr.'s insistence, Ron was regularly drawing on themes from the Arabian Nights and

113

so introducing readers to a world of genies, jinn, Aladdin and Sinbad—all of which, of course, continue to float through cultural mythology to this day.

At least as influential in terms of post-apocalypse stories was L. Ron Hubbard's 1940 *Final Blackout*. Generally acclaimed as the finest anti-war novel of the decade and among the ten best works of the genre ever authored—here, too, was a tale that would live on in ways few other writers

Portland, Oregon, 1943; L. Ron Hubbard captain of the US Navy subchaser PC 815.

imagined. Hence, the later Robert Heinlein verdict: "Final Blackout *is as perfect a piece of science fiction as has ever been written.*"

Like many another who both lived and wrote American pulp adventure, the war proved a tragic end to Ron's sojourn in the pulps. He served with distinction in four theaters and was highly decorated for commanding corvettes in the North Pacific. He was also grievously wounded in combat, lost many a close friend and colleague and thus resolved to say farewell to pulp fiction and devote himself to what it had supported these many years—namely, his serious research.

But in no way was the LRH literary saga at an end, for as he wrote some thirty years later, in 1980:

"Recently there came a period when I had little to do. This was novel in a life so crammed with busy years, and I decided to amuse myself by writing a novel that was pure science fiction."

That work was *Battlefield Earth: A Saga of the Year 3000*. It was an immediate *New York Times* bestseller and, in fact, the first international science fiction blockbuster in decades. It was not, however, L. Ron Hubbard's magnum opus, as that distinction is generally reserved for his next and final work: The 1.2 million word *Mission Earth*.

> **Final Blackout** *is as perfect a piece of science fiction as has ever been written.*
>
> —Robert Heinlein

How he managed those 1.2 million words in just over twelve months is yet another piece of the L. Ron Hubbard legend. But the fact remains, he did indeed author a ten-volume *dekalogy* that lives in publishing history for the fact that each and every volume of the series was also a *New York Times* bestseller.

Moreover, as subsequent generations discovered L. Ron Hubbard through republished works and novelizations of his screenplays, the mere fact of his name on a cover signaled an international bestseller. . . . Until, to date, sales of his works exceed hundreds of millions, and he otherwise remains among the most enduring and widely read authors in literary history. Although as a final word on the tales of L. Ron Hubbard, perhaps it's enough to simply reiterate what editors told readers in the glory days of American Pulp Fiction:

He writes the way he does, brothers, because he's been there, seen it and done it!

THE STORIES FROM THE GOLDEN AGE

Your ticket to adventure starts here with the Stories from
the Golden Age collection by master storyteller L. Ron Hubbard.
These gripping tales are set in a kaleidoscope of exotic locales and brim
with fascinating characters, including some of the
most vile villains, dangerous dames and brazen heroes
you'll ever get to meet.

The entire collection of over one hundred and fifty stories is being
released in a series of eighty books and audiobooks.
For an up-to-date listing of available titles,
go to www.goldenagestories.com.

AIR ADVENTURE

Arctic Wings *Man-Killers of the Air*
The Battling Pilot *On Blazing Wings*
Boomerang Bomber *Red Death Over China*
The Crate Killer *Sabotage in the Sky*
The Dive Bomber *Sky Birds Dare!*
Forbidden Gold *The Sky-Crasher*
Hurtling Wings *Trouble on His Wings*
The Lieutenant Takes the Sky *Wings Over Ethiopia*

FAR-FLUNG ADVENTURE

The Adventure of "X"   *Hurricane*
All Frontiers Are Jealous   *The Iron Duke*
The Barbarians   *Machine Gun 21,000*
The Black Sultan   *Medals for Mahoney*
Black Towers to Danger   *Price of a Hat*
The Bold Dare All   *Red Sand*
Buckley Plays a Hunch   *The Sky Devil*
The Cossack   *The Small Boss of Nunaloha*
Destiny's Drum   *The Squad That Never Came Back*
Escape for Three   *Starch and Stripes*
Fifty-Fifty O'Brien   *Tomb of the Ten Thousand Dead*
The Headhunters   *Trick Soldier*
Hell's Legionnaire   *While Bugles Blow!*
He Walked to War   *Yukon Madness*
Hostage to Death

SEA ADVENTURE

Cargo of Coffins   *The Phantom Patrol*
The Drowned City   *Sea Fangs*
False Cargo   *Submarine*
Grounded   *Twenty Fathoms Down*
Loot of the Shanung   *Under the Black Ensign*
Mister Tidwell, Gunner

TALES FROM THE ORIENT

The Devil—With Wings
The Falcon Killer
Five Mex for a Million
Golden Hell
The Green God
Hurricane's Roar
Inky Odds
Orders Is Orders

Pearl Pirate
The Red Dragon
Spy Killer
Tah
The Trail of the Red Diamonds
Wind-Gone-Mad
Yellow Loot

MYSTERY

The Blow Torch Murder
Brass Keys to Murder
Calling Squad Cars!
The Carnival of Death
The Chee-Chalker
Dead Men Kill
The Death Flyer
Flame City

The Grease Spot
Killer Ape
Killer's Law
The Mad Dog Murder
Mouthpiece
Murder Afloat
The Slickers
They Killed Him Dead

FANTASY

Borrowed Glory   *If I Were You*
The Crossroads   *The Last Drop*
Danger in the Dark   *The Room*
The Devil's Rescue   *The Tramp*
He Didn't Like Cats

SCIENCE FICTION

The Automagic Horse   *A Matter of Matter*
Battle of Wizards   *The Obsolete Weapon*
Battling Bolto   *One Was Stubborn*
The Beast   *The Planet Makers*
Beyond All Weapons   *The Professor Was a Thief*
A Can of Vacuum   *The Slaver*
The Conroy Diary   *Space Can*
The Dangerous Dimension   *Strain*
Final Enemy   *Tough Old Man*
The Great Secret   *240,000 Miles Straight Up*
Greed   *When Shadows Fall*
The Invaders

WESTERN

The Baron of Coyote River
Blood on His Spurs
Boss of the Lazy B
Branded Outlaw
Cattle King for a Day
Come and Get It
Death Waits at Sundown
Devil's Manhunt
The Ghost Town Gun-Ghost
Gun Boss of Tumbleweed
Gunman!
Gunman's Tally
The Gunner from Gehenna
Hoss Tamer
Johnny, the Town Tamer
King of the Gunmen
The Magic Quirt

Man for Breakfast
The No-Gun Gunhawk
The No-Gun Man
The Ranch That No One Would Buy
Reign of the Gila Monster
Ride 'Em, Cowboy
Ruin at Rio Piedras
Shadows from Boot Hill
Silent Pards
Six-Gun Caballero
Stacked Bullets
Stranger in Town
Tinhorn's Daughter
The Toughest Ranger
Under the Diehard Brand
Vengeance Is Mine!
When Gilhooly Was in Flower

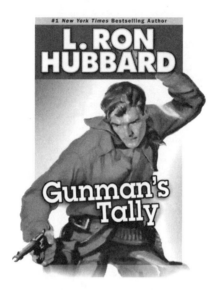

The Magic Quirt

"Aztec! Say, Laramie, there's an Aztec priest lives over by Blue Butte. Regular medicine man he is. Cave full of bats and stone idols. I been over there six, seven times but I never had nerve to go right up to the place. But one day nobody was home and I rid close by and peeked in. And say, it'd make your blood run cold. Stone idols with big green eyes. I bet he makes human sacrifices and everything."

Laramie looked wonderingly at the Kid and then at the quirt. For the first time he saw the design. The handle consisted of a coiled serpent whose head was the top and two great green eyes stared back at him. Suddenly he felt bewitched and thrust the gift from him.

—L. Ron Hubbard

"The 'Golden Age' of Westerns comes to life again."
—*True West*

"Shoot-'em-up action, bad bad guys, heroes cut from the cloth of classic Western heroes, true love, and the final resolution as law and order and justice triumph."
—*KLIATT*

Originally published in the July 1948 issue of *The Rio Kid Western*

ISBN-13 : 978-1-59212-376-6
ISBN-10 : 1-59212-376-7

5 0 9 9 5

9 781592 123766

$9⁹⁵

GALAXY
PRESS

7051 Hollywood Blvd., Suite 200, Hollywood, CA 90028
1-877-8GALAXY (1-877-842-5299)